# PARANORMAL SOLVED

GRACE FLEMING

Three Sheets
PUBLISHING

THREE SHEETS PUBLISHING

Savannah, Georgia

*For my siblings, because we all grew up with those ghosts.*

# THE VOICE OF BAAL

*"Why did you not kill the human?" The voice of Baal came to her from every direction. It seemed to seep from the flames of the fire.*

*The beast's black eyes looked down in shame. They appeared to glow red, as they reflected the dance of the fires that blazed around her.*

*"Did you not enjoy the flesh of the other one?"*

*"I did," she replied. She could not answer the question. She did not know why she did not kill. She had brought great shame to her tribe.*

*"Gaze upon me." The beast knew that the face of Baal had manifested in the fire, but she would not look. She could not. She did not deserve to look at the face of the king.*

*"Why can you not look upon me?"*

*"I do not know," the beast replied. She felt the coolness of a tear on her face, which was now burning hot from the flickering inferno. The tear seemed to draw a loathsome howl from Baal. Oddly, she was not afraid. She would surely be banished, but Gehenna would be a respite compared to the time on earth.*

# 1

## SCHOLARS

"What is up with women's eyebrows lately?" professor Jerry Price asked, as he lazily gazed into the steamy swirl that hovered over his hotel coffee cup. Being the senior member of this group, he felt it was his duty to introduce a little humor. It was the third day of the research conference, and Jerry wasn't sure he could make it to the end without ripping off a big snore in the middle of somebody's presentation. "I had to tell my wife she drew hers on too high." The two men across the table just stared back at him with sleepy eyes, until Josh White, the youngest of the three academics, gave in.

"Really? What did she say?"

Jerry rubbed at his grey speckled mustache, as if deep in thought for a moment. "She looked surprised," he said.

Jerry threw his head back and let out a laugh that might have been a little too loud for the other attendees in the conference center breakfast room, but he just couldn't believe the kid had fallen for the old joke. He was rewarded by the fact that Josh was giggling back at him, his face bright red and still puffy from the early morning hangover.

"You are such a moron," the third man at the table said, as his brooding, dark eyes darted apologetically around the room. David Blystone was the most serious of the three, and if Jerry could be honest, the man could use a helping hand when it came to pulling the big stick out of his ass.

"Let's give him a break," Josh said. "I mean, I think that's the first time I've cracked a smile all week. Yesterday I sat for an hour and a half learning how to build a decision tree."

"It's a *research* conference," David said. "It's not supposed to be titivating." He stirred at his own cup of black tea for a second before speaking again. "But you're right. This conference is basically as boring as shit."

"Thank god," Jerry said, feeling relieved to know that the others were nearly as miserable as he was. He could be just as serious as anybody else when it came to researching and writing, but this conference was verging on torture. "Three days is just too much for such a dry topic. I know all I ever wanted to know about qualitative and quantitative methodologies. I say we ditch this place and go exploring a little. I'd like to see some historic stuff while I'm here. I hear there's an old oyster shucking museum."

David stared blankly back at Jerry, while Josh held an imaginary gun to his head and pulled the trigger. Obviously, his friends didn't understand the rich cultural significance of such a place. But then, they were scientists.

"Can we think of something else, before I pluck out my eyelashes for amusement?" David said.

Jerry scrunched his face in response, but neither of his friends noticed. They both seemed to be staring past Jerry's shoulder, gazing wide-eyed at something going on in the large lobby outside the breakfast room. He twisted his body around and glanced out the wide open doors, but he didn't see anything.

"*Did you see what just walked by*?" Josh laughed and jumped to his feet. He was looking around the room and pointing into the lobby. David was laughing, as were a few other people in the room.

Jerry hated being on the outside of a good laugh. He scanned the big hallway, but he was coming up empty. Just the usual bustle of people mulling around with name badges hanging from their lanyards. "What was it?" he said. But as the words left his lips, he spotted the apparent source of his friends' amusement. On the far corner of the grand lobby, a woman was waiting for her turn on the busy elevator. She was struggling to balance a large sign with the words GHOSTS AND SHADOW PEOPLE printed in red letters. Below the words, there was a large arrow pointing to the right.

Josh pushed his empty chair into place at the round table. "I have to follow that woman," he said. "I gotta see what that's about."

Jerry watched as Josh jogged across the lobby, making his way to the far side just in time to board the elevator with the sign-bearing woman. He envied the kid's youthful enthusiasm. Jerry could tell he was struggling to keep a straight face as he attempted to engage the woman in conversation.

"Well, it wouldn't be Savannah if we didn't see something weird," David sighed, as he sipped at his tea. He'd apparently recovered from his brief lapse into cheerfulness.

"Exactly!" Jerry said. "We can't spend three whole days in this city and not enjoy any of its oddness. It would be a crime. We've got to find a way to ditch this conference and catch a tour or something, while the dean is busy with her meetings."

"I dunno," David said. "Maybe we could find some trendy cafe and hang out. Maybe find some hot moms."

That was David in a nutshell, Jerry thought. He was a pretty simple guy. Basically, there were two extreme sides to the guy's personality: nerdiness and lechery. Jerry found David's skirt chasing to be a bore, but only because he, himself, had never found any other woman attractive since he'd met his current wife. But then, David had never achieved a serious relationship, either. He was handsome enough, with his dark hair and near-black eyes; he was just as boring as a slug race most of the time. Jerry realized that he might need to sneak off on his own if he really wanted to enjoy himself at all in Savannah, and he was hatching a plan when he noticed that Josh was strutting back across the lobby toward them with a beaming grin.

"You guys won't believe this," he said as he approached the table. "Guess what's taking place on the second floor?"

"Some kind of costume thing?" David said. "Lots of people get into those."

"A paranormal convention," Josh said, sounding like he'd just discovered a new continent.

Jerry looked at David to observe his reaction, and he was relieved to see that the man was also baffled. "What the hell are they doing up there?" Jerry asked. "Like, a giant séance?"

"Nope. It's not just ghost stuff." Josh was sitting on the edge of his chair, chattering like an excited child. "There's all these rooms with signs in front of them. Apparently, they have lectures, like we do at our conference. Only their topics are things like ghosts, Bigfoot, and aliens. It's aweso—" Josh's last word was interrupted by his own abrupt laugh. "You guys need to go check it out."

To Jerry's surprise, David's face had softened into a smile. "Seriously?" he said.

"And you should get a look at the Bigfoot presenter," Josh said. "That woman is unbelievable."

"You mean in a good way?" David asked. Apparently, the kid knew exactly how to pique the interest of the dark-eyed biologist.

"I mean in an underwear model kind of way," Josh answered. He fashioned his hands into cup shapes and hovered them over his chest.

"That's it, I'm in," David said, as he jumped to his feet. "You coming?" David and Josh stared down at Jerry.

The thought of a museum really did appeal to Jerry. But he could always slip out later, when he became bored. "I'm right behind you," he said.

## 2

## OBSERVATION AND PARTICIPATION

Jerry huddled in a metal chair in the third row of a near-empty room, bent down with his phone pressed to his ear to avoid the off chance that anyone in the hallway would hear him. One other man sat alone near the back of the room, appearing to be absorbed in some booklet. Like Jerry, the man was waiting for the next lecture to begin. It was scheduled to start in fifteen minutes.

"I feel like I'm in a crazy factory," he whispered to his wife on the other end of the phone. "They all walk around here looking very serious, like it's a real conference. I swear, some people will believe anything!"

"Jerry," Vivian Price said on the other end of the line, her voice not sounding at all as amused as Jerry had hoped. "You can't get into trouble at the university for this, could you? I mean, what would the dean say? Does she know what you're up to? She used a lot of her budget money to foot the bill for this little trip."

"Not yet," Jerry said. "But I'm not alone. Josh and David are doing it too."

"Are you serious? I can't believe David would go along with this. You and Josh, yes. But not David."

"I don't think we have to worry about David," Jerry said. "He got his first choice of sessions. You know that really hot chick who stars in that Bigfoot show?"

"You mean *Sasquatch Encounters*? Laura London is there?" Vivian sounded impressed. It wasn't that either of them actually watched a Bigfoot show, themselves. But their son did, and Jerry and Vivian just happened to catch a few scenes now and then.

"She's here, alright. You should see everyone following her around."

"Wait, what is your session about?" Vivian asked.

Jerry paused for a moment. He had a feeling that Vivian wouldn't approve of his selected topic, but something about it made Jerry curious. "The title is "Demons and Cryptids," Jerry said. "It sounded sexy."

"You are kidding me!" Vivian's voice was no longer the gentle, soothing tone he was used to. "That sounds horrifying!" The words sounded through his phone just as a few audience members entered the room. "Jerry, honey, I don't have a good feeling about this."

"*Sshhh*," he chuckled as he whispered into the phone. "You'll get me busted!"

"Are you sure you won't get caught?"

"It'll be fine," Jerry whispered through a fake smile. "You know Crystal is a cool boss." He was starting to regret calling his wife now. He'd expected her to get a good laugh out of this, but he should have known she'd worry. "And, besides," he continued. "We plan to tell her all about it tonight, over drinks."

"I just hope she doesn't fire you all. I know she's pretty chill, but she doesn't always get your humor, you know."

"We'd have to do something pretty bad to get fired," Jerry laughed. We have tenure." He looked up to see two men hovering around the doorway, looking in to make sure they were about to enter the right room. "I'd better go," he said into the phone. "People are coming in."

He watched as a mix of people started to amble into the room. They all looked pretty normal, so far, although he wasn't sure what he'd expected them to look like. He checked his conference name badge and twisted the lanyard around backward to hide the imprint, making sure that nobody could spot him as an intruder, when a tall, elderly man entered the room. He had a curly white crop of hair on his head that matched the equally white beard. The distinguished looking man nodded at several audience members as he made his way to the front of the room, toward a podium and a small raised stage.

"How are you?" the man said as he passed by Jerry. Jerry just nodded in response. He was half expecting everyone to break out in laughter and tell him this was all a joke. He'd managed to read a little bit about the speaker since he'd made the decision to crash the session. Apparently, this gentleman in the front of the room fancied himself an expert on cryptids of all sorts. Jerry wrote the words "chupacabra whisperer" on his note pad. The guys would crack up at that, later. He kept his eye on the man to see if he seemed to give off any eye signals to some secret co-conspirator in the audience, but the man just stood erect with his arms crossed in front of him and nodded as the room now filled rapidly. Someone in the back of the room rang a small bell, which signaled starting time. Once everyone settled into a seat, the man started to speak.

"As you may know by now, I am Dr. Johan Nilsson, and I am originally from Stockholm." Jerry wondered if the accent was real. People always fell for a good accent. "I'd like to start off by learning a little bit about you all," the man continued.

Jerry sunk lower into his chair. The last thing he wanted to do was introduce himself and have to come up with a lie about why he was there. He brainstormed for a fake name for several seconds before he realized he was being silly. Surely, the man didn't actually intend for every person in the room to tell a personal story. To his relief, the man confirmed this.

"I'll ask a few questions and you can answer if you feel comfortable," the speaker said. "I'll just jump right in and ask the obvious one we'd all like to discuss. Has anyone in the room actually seen or had a first hand experience with any type of mysterious entity, whatever you may call them, be it gnomes, fairies, or the like?"

Jerry twisted around to see if anyone would actually speak up. A man in a red sweater sitting in the back of the room slowly lifted his hand. "I have," he said sheepishly. Everyone contorted their bodies and twisted in their metal chairs to take a look at the poor man.

"Do you feel comfortable sharing your experience with everyone?" Dr. Nilsson asked. "There's absolutely no pressure."

"It's fine," the man said. "There's not much to tell."

Jerry could hardly hear the man from the distance of the long room, and he was glad to hear several audience members urging the guy to speak up. Apparently, nobody wanted to miss this.

"It happened so fast," the sweater man said, "that I have almost convinced myself that I am remembering wrong. I was walking through a dense patch of woods in Pennsylvania, where I used to live, when I turned a corner to see a little—creature, standing there. It was the weirdest thing, he had a look of shock on his face, as did I, I'm pretty sure. He just stared right at me for a minute and ran off into the woods, and that was that. I didn't see anything of him after that, but I was absolutely positive that I saw a humanoid, or whatever you want to call it, that day. And I can promise you that I had never believed anything like that existed before-hand. And, no, I wasn't drinking."

The room filled with nervous giggles.

"What did he look like?" someone from the group asked.

The sweater man rolled his eyes upward and rubbed his chin, as if to conjure the vision in his head. "He looked like a stocky man, really, but one who only stood about two feet high. And I hesitate to say this, and it's why I never normally tell anybody...it just sounds so ridiculous..." The man paused, seemingly searching for words—or courage.

"Go on," the professor said.

"Well, I feel quite crazy divulging this bit. I've never told this to anyone outside this room. He was naked, for one thing." He paused again. "The creature's skin was see-through. I could see skeleton and organs. It was just horri-ble, really."

Several murmurs came from the audience, but Dr. Nilsson nodded knowingly. "I'm sure it was," he said in a soothing tone. "I'm sure it was."

"Well, that's all there is to it," the man said. "I'm sorry it's not a very exciting story, but I sure haven't ever forgotten it." Jerry looked around the room where several mouths were hanging open. For a brief time, the room was silent.

"Well, I'm so glad you shared your story," the doctor said, "And I can assure you that you are not crazy, and you are not alone."

"Thank you," the man said as he lowered himself into his chair. "So you really believe me?"

"I certainly do," Dr. Nilsson said, as he held up a figure. "As a matter of fact, I know exactly who—or what it was—that you saw. If you'd like to chat a bit more after this presentation, I'd be glad to talk with you later."

The man looked as if he were gazing into the eyes of his savior, and Jerry made a mental note that they guy was either a great actor, or he really believed the ordeal he'd just described. The man's eyes glistened with tears after Dr. Nilsson's words of comfort.

Jerry remembered that he was supposed to be taking detailed written notes for his friends, so he wrote furiously to make sure he described every word and observation from the man's story. As he wrote, he half-listened to Dr. Nilsson describing the different characteristics of this creature and that, and explaining the geographical sightings of several known types. He scribbled to keep up with the lecturer, when he heard the man throwing out another question to the audience.

"Do you think demons are real?" he asked. This time, an uncomfortable silence fell over the room, and several people raised their hands, nervously. "I have a reason for asking, of course," Nilsson said. "In my next book, I shall detail my theory that many of the cryptids that people are seeing and experiencing around the world, are, in fact, the entities that we commonly understand to be demons. But before I go further, let me present to you some rather surprising facts." He paused and looked around for effect. "Ten years ago, the Michigan area was menaced by a terrifying creature with the head of a wolf and the body of a large, muscular human. Today, this creature, commonly called Dogman, has been reported in at least twenty states, in England, and in Australia."

Several audience members reacted, to the great satisfaction of the presenter, Jerry noticed. "Sounds like a werewolf," a voice shouted from behind Jerry.

"Many people do believe this creature to be a werewolf," Nilsson responded. "But Dogman is not the only cryptid to be showing up in increasing numbers. For years, people in West Virginia reported Mothman encounters. Did you know that a very similar creature has been frequently sighted in Mexico? And those well known creatures aren't the only ones showing up in large numbers. Pterodactyl sightings are on the rise, lizard people are seen across the country, and wendigos, once a creature of the Great Lakes region, are showing up in forests across the South, to the horror of hunters and hikers, as one can imagine."

At this point, Jerry managed to stifle an involuntary groan, just in time. The man's claims were getting more and more fantastical now, and Jerry was just about to retire his note-taking pen when a rapid, floor-level flash of movement caused him to turn his head to the right. Dr. Nilsson must have seen it, too, because he hesitated for a moment and looked in the same direction. There was nothing there, but Jerry could swear he had seen a flicker of color and light. It had been a mere dash of movement; just enough to grab the attention of anyone who happened to be sitting near the front row.

*This is rich*, Jerry thought. The tricks are beginning. Dr. Nilsson had spent the last twenty minutes setting the stage, and now he was about to start the show with some visual trickery. He'd probably used this method a hundred times before. Jerry stopped listening to the man's narrative and focused, instead, on finding the method of his chicanery. He twisted around to look for anything like a duct or protrusion that could conceal a small projector. There was a device hanging from the ceiling, of course, the type of thing you can always find in conference rooms. It was a projector designed specifically for slide presentations, though, and it was turned off. It wasn't designed to project flashes and flickering lights around the edges of the floor to trick audience members into thinking they'd seen a creature of some kind, lurking in the perimeters of the room.

The flicker he'd seen was so obvious a trick that Jerry felt sorry for the audience members. But then, nobody else seemed the least bit distracted, which was curious. Maybe it was designed so that only one or two people near the front of the room could see something odd? That would certainly arouse excitement and, at the same time, build up a sense of eagerness in the ones who didn't experience a vision. Either way, Jerry was determined to figure out what was really happening here. He scanned the walls and the edges of the ceiling looking for tiny openings.

A searing pain in his right calf made him jump, and he glanced down to see if he'd bumped into some sharp object. The thing he saw was so unexpected that he let out an involuntary *yelp*! There, standing right beside his leg, was something so strange and horrible looking, that Jerry forgot where he was for a time. His eyes fell on something so— sickening, and so filled with pure hate, that he stood up suddenly. The thing was making a hissing sound. As he tried to stand, everything around him went dark, and a sickening smell wafted up his nostrils. "What the f—?" he blurted and stumbled to the side at the same time, but as quick as the words left his mouth, the light returned and the vision disappeared. The interruption caused Dr. Nilsson to stop talking and glare in Jerry's direction.

"Did you just see something?" Dr. Nilsson asked.

*For shit's sake,* Jerry thought. He was seething, but he wasn't about to let it show to the audience. His leg now hurt like hell, but he was not about to cooperate with this ridiculous parlor game and give Dr. Nilsson the satisfaction of going along with his tricks. "No," Jerry said. "I just sneezed and it caused my back to spasm. Sorry for the interruption." He hoped the man could tell that he was seething. He stared into Nilsson's eyes, hoping to convey the rage he was feeling, as he settled back into his chair.

Dr. Nilsson just stared back at him for a moment, before directing his attention to the entire audience. "I want to take this opportunity to make a very serious request." He paused for several seconds, and Jerry assumed it was for dramatic effect. "If anyone hears or sees anything out of the ordinary, I want you to let me know. I'm very serious. Please come and speak with me after the presentation if you have an experience." His face turned more somber and he looked directly at Jerry. "I'm saying this for your own good."

*Good God,* Jerry thought. The man was desperate for him to play along, but Jerry wasn't about to give him an inch. He had no idea what the man was doing to make him see and feel odd things, but he wasn't going to let the man make a fool of him. He'd seen enough TV magic shows to know that this was elementary level trickery. Hell, Jerry half expected people to pop in with cameras for a big reveal and lots of laughs and slaps on the back. He'd wait out the man in the front of the room until this show was over, and he'd remain cool until that time. *But his leg was burning with pain.*

He'd lost track of what the man was talking about now, and he was writing furiously about the vision he'd seen. He was dying to raise his pant leg enough to see if there was a puncture on his calf, and he could swear he felt a blood trickle on his ankle. The son of a bitch in the front of the room had gone to great lengths to convince some poor bastard in the audience that his gimmick was real, but the theatrics were lost on Jerry. Jesus, no wonder people had to dish out a lot of money to attend this carnival. There was some impressive technology behind this shit, or some advanced psychological tricks, but he didn't want to give this man an ounce of satisfaction. He was writing as the thoughts came to him, and realized that his pen was quivering in his hand.

He heard people speaking behind him again, and realized it was Q&A time. The whole fiasco would be finished in a few minutes, Jerry told himself, and then he would be headed for drinks and beers with his co-workers.

## 3

## INTERDISCIPLINARY STUDIES

"Shhhh, don't say anything," Jerry said to the other men at the bar table as Crystal Nixon, Dean of the College of Arts and Sciences, entered the hotel lounge. "Let's not tell her until we've filled her with a few shots of bourbon. I hope your sessions were good. Were they good?"

"I thought we weren't supposed to say anything," Josh said as he scooted a stool to make room for another seat at the table.

"I don't want any details, jerk," Jerry whispered. I just wanted to know if your session was interesting. Mine was outrageous. I'd like to kill the bastard who ran my session." He reached his hand down to massage the back of his calf, which was burning like it was on fire.

"Oh, my session was interesting." Josh said, seemingly oblivious to Jerry's words. "Like, insane."

"Mine, too," David whispered quickly, twirling his finger beside his temple in a "crazy" gesture, just before Crystal approached the table.

The woman lunged herself onto the high stool and sat for a

second, looking around at each face. "What the hell are you three up to?" she said as she pulled the table toward her to make a loud screeching sound. "I know those faces. What's going on?"

Jerry could see the look of guilt on the faces of his two friends, and he assumed his face was also a dead giveaway. "Um, can you have a drink, first?" he asked. Even though Crystal was the coolest boss ever, she was still a boss. He was suddenly feeling less confident than he had before. Crystal had spent a lot of the year's travel budget bringing them all to the research conference, and they were about to confess that they had ditched it to have some silly fun.

"Spill it," she said.

"Well," David stammered. "We have a confession, but it's all these guys' fault. I'm the serious guy, remember?"

Oh, really?" Jerry said in his most taunting voice. "You're the one who ditched us for the hot chick."

Crystal responded with a threatening glare. Now Jerry was really starting to wonder if they'd all gone too far. "Okay," he said. "Just hear me out. You have to admit that this is the most boring damned conference you've ever experienced. I mean, we're hearing the same shit over and over again, am I wrong?"

"It's a bit boring, yes." She nodded her head in concession. "Now what have you done?"

"I may as well jump right in," Josh said. "I'm partly to blame, since it was my discovery. We all thought it would be funny to crash a paranormal convention."

"A *what*?" Crystal said as she looked around the table. She seemed more confused than angered.

"There was a gathering of paranormal enthusiasts on the floor above us," Josh explained, as if he was stating the most obvious thing in the world. "Me, David, and Jerry all picked different topics and agreed to check it out and report back what we heard. I guess it was stupid."

"Somebody please buy me a beer, right now," Crystal said.

○─○

JERRY RETURNED from his strategically timed trip to the men's room, which was designed, admittedly, to let the others defend their collective foolery in his absence. Hell, Jerry was a year from retiring, and seniority had to count for something, so he left his colleagues with the task of explaining their decidedly unprofessional behavior. He'd used the time to take a look at the sore place on his leg, which now appeared to have two small holes that were swelling up and throbbing. He'd have to run out later to get some ointment and bandages, which was a huge pain in the ass. But for now, he was determined not to show that anything was wrong. He approached the table cautiously, trying to read his boss's mood, and he was relieved to see that she was sporting a relaxed smile, along with the others.

"So are we in trouble?" Jerry said, as he climbed onto the tall stool.

"I haven't decided," Crystal said, as she finished a long chug and wiped her mouth with her sleeve. "But you may as well tell me what happened, now that it's done. This should be good."

"David first," Jerry said. "He can tell us about Bigboobs. I mean Bigfoot." Jerry was proud to see that Crystal spit a little beer across the table.

David pressed his hands to the side of his face as if to hide a blush. "Oh, that was clever," he said. "But here's a shocker. It appears that she—the Bigfoot hunter I went to see—actually has a brain."

"As if you'd notice," Jerry said. "So did you manage to hear anything she had to say or did you spend the whole hour concentrating on her—greatness?"

David settled his beer bottle and scratched at the label nervously. "Well, it was interesting," he started. "She certainly is more famous than I knew, with her TV show and all. The people freakin loved her." Jerry watched the faces of his friends, and they looked intrigued. "And she certainly came across like she believed every word she said. And she's actually got an Ivy League degree, by the way."

"No shit?" Josh blurted.

"I knew that," Jerry said. "From the show. They claim she's the real deal when it comes to smarts."

"Apparently." David said. "And I was kind of impressed with her genuine demeanor. She seems to really believe what she's saying, and she has a lot of friends at big time research institutions. It's weird. It seems her interest began when she was a young girl living in some remote part of Oklahoma. She claims to have seen some big hairy monster who visited their property a few times, and she claims it killed her horse."

"Crazy!" Crystal said.

"I know," David continued. "I'm telling you, she was convincing, that's for damn sure. And as for the crowd, it was mostly listeners. There was only one guy, other than Laura, who claimed to have had an encounter. Mostly, Laura was talking about the scientific evidence they had that 'proved' some unknown primate was running around in the woods. Things like footprint patterns and DNA samples." David took a long swig of beer. "But then it all got a little strange during the Q&A time," he paused to belch. "When people started talking about other types of cryptos running around out there. Some guy said there was a dog-like man running around in the swamp behind his farm in South Carolina. It felt kind of awkward, listening to that one. I mean, come on, man."

"That's Dogman," Jerry said. " I know all about this stuff. Ask me anything." He couldn't help grinning as he took a swig from his mug.

"Well, just when you were about to make me a believer," Crystal said, looking around the table. "Not really," she added, which caused a relieved ripple of laughter.

"Other than that," David continued, " there was some talk about upcoming fact finding expeditions in the Northwest. They actually sounded kind of fun. But I have to say as a lover of statistics, I could prove in a few short minutes that it is impossible for an animal of that size to survive without detection. Sad. I sort of wish I could believe some of the stories. A big human-like species running around in the woods is kind of a cool thought. But that's about it for my session."

"Well, I'll go ahead and go next," Josh spoke up, "because I'm not nearly so melancholy about the folks at my session. I mean, those folks were just batshit crazy."

It was obvious from the chuckles around the table that the alcohol was having its desired effect on the group. As the usual center of attention, Jerry was kind of envious of the reaction the others were getting.

"So I chose alien abduction, just as a reminder. I was sitting there about ten minutes before I heard the first 'I woke up to find myself on a spaceship' story. I mean, half the damn people in the room had been to outer space, by the sound of it." There was another spurt of chuckles around the table as Josh unfolded a slip of note paper and donned a pair of glasses. "Let's see," he said, as he read over his notes. "Everyone had pretty much the same thing to say. 'I was floating through the air, I woke up on an operating table, I saw a little man with big eyes, they implanted something under my skin.' That was pretty much what I heard, over and over again."

"Interesting," Crystal said. "What do you suppose would make them say or believe such a thing?"

"Oh, I'm pretty sure I could come up with a few explanations," Josh said. "Mass hysteria is a real thing, you know."

"So, that was it?" Jerry asked. His story sounded sort of generic so far.

"Pretty much," Josh said, as he looked over his note paper. "Oh, there was this one lady. She apparently had a set of twins after being impregnated by the aliens. One lives with her, but the other lives in space."

Everyone but Jerry was laughing. Nobody else was claiming any elaborate tactics like he'd experienced in his session. Jerry had gone over several possibilities in his head, like maybe the possibility that he'd undergone some sort of hypnosis, and the thing he'd seen was really a cat or a dog, which his brain had interpreted as a creature—or whatever. The animal had likely been trained to bite, but some sort of trickery of the mind, like power of suggestion, had been enacted to make him "see" something entirely different.

"So what about Jerry the demon guy?" Josh taunted. "What do you have to say for your session?"

Jerry was still not sure what he was going to say to the others. He wasn't entirely comfortable sharing everything he'd experienced. He was having a hard time keeping the terrible vision out of his head. Just the thought of it made him feel a little sick.

"Well, it was interesting," he said. "Like the others, I was trapped in a room full of, let's say, ardent believers." He pulled his own notes from his shirt pocket and looked them over before continuing. "It was really just a tease for a book the guy was writing." He'd decided not to elaborate about his experience just yet. "There are different categories of little critters, you see, and in this particular session, the speaker explained that most of them—things like elves and green lizard men—are really demons."

"That was it? A boring book talk?" Josh was apparently disappointed.

"Hardly boring," Jerry said. He resented the implication that his session was lame. "The guy provided an overview of the most common monsters people see, and then threw in a few garden gnomes, like those you may have seen at your grandmother's house. Elves, gnomes, fairies, and the like. They're all demonic, and they can only be seen by a select few, I've learned."

"Well, that's convenient," Josh moaned.

"Right," Jerry said. "But as it turns out, I apparently have the gift."

The words left everyone staring blankly at Jerry.

"I saw one," he said. It might have been the alcohol taking effect, but he now decided to go for it. Everyone leaned forward to listen to what he would say next. "It's true. I was the lone audience member sitting close to the front row, and I saw something. We all endured about twenty minutes of lecture about the history of weirdness—and then the tricks began. It started when I saw a flicker of movement out of the corner of my eye. Some little trick of light, I assume. Then, a little later, I actually saw something."

"That's freakin' crazy!" Crystal shouted. Even for a bar, it was a little loud. She was also enjoying her drink, it seemed.

"You have to be shitting me," Josh said. "How the hell did the guy manage that?

"I have no idea," Jerry said. He was enjoying the limelight. "I looked around for hidden projectors and such, but I didn't see anything obvious. I don't know if it was suggestion that made me see it, or if it was some kind of 3-D projection —I'm not sure. I have to say, I thought for the longest time that you all were messing with me—like it was some kind of setup. I actually expected you all to come busting through the door."

"What did it look like?" David asked. His rumpled face was suspended in an incredulous stare.

"Just exactly like a yard gnome," Jerry lied. For some reason, he didn't feel like describing what he really saw. "It even had pointy ears."

"Oh, bullshit," Josh said. "What fantastic bullshit. If I was going to trick somebody into thinking they saw an elf, I wouldn't make it *look* exactly like an elf. You know what I mean? What bullshit."

"I know," Jerry said. "It was nuts. But that's what happened. I'd love to figure out what that son of a bitch did. Did I tell you it bit me?" He was so intoxicated by the beer and the attention, that he couldn't remember if he'd divulged this particular detail.

"Noooo...," Crystal said, looking at the others from the corner of her eye. Jerry realized he was starting to sound like one of the crazy ones. By the look on her face, and the looks coming from David and Josh, he decided against elaborating about the details. In fact, he wasn't even sure why he claimed he was bitten. He didn't actually see what had happened to his leg.

"I just felt a sting on my leg, that's all. Some weird kind

of power of suggestion going on. I don't know what he did, but I'd love to find out."

The silence that followed made Jerry feel a bit ridiculous, like the rest of them were judging him for believing he really felt something.

"Well, you're going to, right?" The silence was broken by David.

"Going to what?" Crystal said. Her voice was starting to slur a little, but no more than anyone else's. "Go after the little demon guy? Kick his ass?"

"Not just that," David said, with the bravado that usually follows several beers. "I'm thinking we might spend some more time looking into all of this. Each of us could try to figure out what makes these people believe what they do."

"Why would we?" Josh asked.

"Well," David said in his best professorly voice. "Here's the problem: people like this—the people who believe in paranormal shit—they perpetuate the dangerous notion that science isn't reliable. They believe in these stories without any kind of real evidence to back up their claims, and that's just dangerous for humanity. We're all intelligent, here. Maybe we can figure out what kind of tricks and mind play goes on to make these people believe what they do."

"Wait. You're planning on going on a camping trip with the Sasquatch lady, aren't you?" Josh asked. Jerry wished he'd thought of that first. Everybody was laughing.

"Well, she *has* invited me," David said sheepishly. "I mean, spending the summer in a sleeping bag with a beautiful woman isn't exactly the worst offer I've ever had."

"You dirty bastard," Jerry said.

"But, seriously. I think we can really make a serious study of our topics and maybe do lots of conferences about the fallibility of personal testimony. It would be a kick ass study. We could examine the claims of the folks who really believe in the different topics, then explain what's really going on, whether it's a case of suggestion, or mass hysteria, or tricks of light, or all of the above. We could bring it back to the research conference next year! We could at least liven up next year's meeting. I think people would love it!"

Jerry was glad David was enthusiastic about the topic. He wanted to nail the white-haired bastard from his own session. "I'm game," he said.

"I have to admit that I'm intrigued by the number of people who believe they've experienced abduction," Josh said. "I'll play if you guys do. I don't have a lot planned for this summer."

"What about me?" Crystal said. "What do I get?"

"Seriously?" Jerry said. He could hardly believe that his boss was willing to go along with such a crazy idea, although it did have potential as a great presentation at next year's conference.

"Sure," she said. "I wanna play."

"We're in Savannah," Josh said. "What about ghosts?"

## 4

## OPERATIONS RESEARCH

J osh placed himself in a dark corner of the airport seating area. He didn't want the others to know what he was up to, just in case they weren't actually serious about this new project idea. He got enough ribbing from them, so he didn't want to take the risk of being the butt of another joke.

He pushed his earplugs into place and twisted his body around to make double sure that his back was to a wall. When he was certain that no one was within range to see what he was up to, he opened the lid to his laptop. He'd seen the video a few times before, but for some reason, he wanted to watch it again and again.

He enlarged the video to fill his screen. There were a few seconds of fuzzy jerking motions before an image started to emerge. It was hazy at first, but gradually, the camera light adjusted, so a pastoral image took form, showing several brown cattle of all sizes. They were dozing in a pasture, all huddled in a small group. There was no sound to accompany the video. The silence made the scene seem eerie.

Suddenly, there was a brief, bright flash of light to make

the screen go white. When the cows came back into view, it appeared that a few of the animals had attempted to bolt, but they stopped, abruptly. They were encircled in light, and they appeared to be frozen into place, except for their eyes. Their faces were all locked into twisted grimaces, but their eyes were darting wildly. They had the look of terror.

After a moment, there was one small movement that came from the center of the group. It was a small calf, and it stumbled around a bit, appearing to struggle for its balance. In the next moment, it appeared that the calf was jumping, but the unnatural movement of its legs revealed that the calf was, instead, rising from the ground.

Josh was mesmerized as he watched the calf rise into the air. Slowly, it lifted as its body twisted wildly, upward it moved toward what now seemed to be the source of the soft light. Josh watched until the calf disappeared into the top of his screen.

He closed his laptop and slipped it into its case. He knew exactly how and where he would spend his summer.

## 5

## UNEXPECTED FINDINGS

"What's for supper?"

Jerry could smell the familiar aroma of his favorite meal as he came in the front door of his home after the long drive from the airport. The truth was, he knew before he got out of the car what he'd be having for dinner. Any time he was away from his house for more than a day, which wasn't that often, his wife treated him with her special chili with shredded cheese and corn chips—even if it was a warm outside, like today. But he had to act like he was surprised, so she could chastise him for forgetting. Neither of them would dream of disappointing the other when it came to their rituals.

"You silly old fool," she yelled from the kitchen. "Crank up the air, it's chili night!"

This was another part of their homecoming ritual. Jerry had to lower the thermostat until the digital numbers counted down to 67 degrees inside the house, so they could pretend it was wintertime and curl up together on the sofa to watch a movie. It was the only way to enjoy summertime chili.

"Give us a kiss," he said as he wandered into the kitchen where he knew he'd find her hovering over a stove, stirring a large pot. It never got old, coming home to this woman. From her spiky, dark-rooted hair to her tattooed white ankles, he loved every inch of her.

It had taken him two attempts, but he had found the woman of his dreams nearly ten years earlier, and they'd never grown tired of spending time together. He'd hardly been able to believe his luck the first time she'd agreed to go out with him. He was a poor graduate student at Ohio State when he bumped into Vivian, a part time art history lecturer, in the small upstairs room of the library that was set aside for special collections. Jerry had been fascinated to learn that Vivian's grandfather had worked as an aide to John Kennedy, and the two of them had hit it off immediately. Jerry was going through a messy, painful divorce at the time, but meeting her that evening was the new beginning that he'd so desperately needed, and after suffering three horrific years in a dysfunctional, twisted union filled with drugs and bouts of rage, the chance encounter in the library had saved his sanity.

"How was your trip?" she asked, while twisting her right cheek toward him to receive his kiss. "Anything interesting happen?"

"Don't ask," he mumbled. He'd been dwelling on the bizarre conference incident all day, but he still wasn't comfortable enough to open up about it. The more he'd thought about the weird incident at the conference, the more the whole thing bothered him. Not only did the vision of the strange little creature leave a vivid image in his mind, but the wound in his leg seemed to be growing redder and more painful. He wasn't sure how to process everything yet, so he wanted to give it more time before he confided in

Vivian. He pulled a clean spoon from a drawer and scooped a sample bite of chili from the bubbling pot. Although he'd expected a swift swat on the arm and some push back for his behavior, he realized that Vivian seemed preoccupied by her own thoughts. She wasn't behaving normally. He pulled a chair from the small kitchenette and settled into a seat. "I'd rather hear about your day," he said.

Vivian tapped the wooden spoon on the edge of the pot and stared intently downward. "I think you'll need to sit down," she said. "I've got something to tell you."

"I'm already sitting," Jerry said. A sick feeling was starting to swill in his gut. It wasn't like her to be so distant. "What is it?"

"Please don't be too upset, honey," she said as she turned to finally face him. "I know you'll be disappointed, but Luke won't be joining us tonight."

"That's it?" he said. He loved his son and all, but he didn't mind him going out with friends. He wasn't naive enough to expect him to stay his best pal forever. He was a teen now.

"That's not quite all." Vivian walked over to join him at the table and slid into a chair next to him. "It's Karen. She's decided she wants to *spend some time* with him." Her voice was thick with sarcasm.

The words had a noxious effect. After years of merciful silence, his irrational, self-destructive and quite insane ex-wife had decided to enter the scene to try her hand at motherhood, once again. It was the last thing he needed to hear. "Oh my god," he said, burying his head in his hands.

"Listen," Vivian said as she smacked the back of his hand. "She's crazy, I know, but things are a little bit different, now. He's not five years old. At least Luke is old enough to look out for himself if she goes on a drug binge or forgets that he's in the house."

"Don't remind me," Jerry said. "He rubbed between his eyes to relieve the tension he suddenly felt.

"And I'm sorry I didn't stop him from going," Vivian said. "You were already in flight and she just showed up at the door. Poor Luke didn't know how to act, but he did seem like he was happy to go with her. I didn't have any right to stop her, you know."

"I know," Jerry said. He felt for his wife, who didn't deserve to have to deal with his ex, although she had been forced to deal with her several times. "And you're right, the boy is old enough, now, that I don't have to be terrified that she'll leave him at the grocery store or something worse. Thank god I got him that phone. Now he can call me if she goes off."

"That's right. He's old enough to look out for himself and call us if he needs us. But there's something else."

"What?" Jerry said. He braced himself for a horrific twist. He'd known Karen for a long time and he knew that nothing was out of the question when it came to his ex. "What else?"

"Well, she's apparently managed to marry someone, and the poor soul she married seems to be loaded. She came in here with an armload of gifts and she said she's living on a farm with horses. That's why he was so willing to go with her. Maybe he'll have a good time."

Jerry let out a deep, involuntary sigh. He thought he was having a weird day already, but now things had taken another unwelcome twist. "What did I do to deserve this?" he said.

"Come on, now," Vivian said, as she pushed away from the table. "I'm not going to let this ruin our night. Go get cleaned up for dinner and I'll find us a movie. Let's make the most of this night."

She'd always had a way of cheering him up, and tonight

was no different. When he thought about it, he was relieved that things were much different now that Luke was older. Years ago, when he'd had to let Karen go off with Luke, there were so many possibilities that terrified him and kept him awake all night. She really was a walking disaster, and she had done some pretty stupid and mindless things to put their son in real danger. But it was different now. He had to believe that. And perhaps Luke deserved to get to know his mother now, even though he might not like what he finds. He'd had this discussion with Vivian a few times, and they'd both known that this moment was coming. Luke would get curious, or Karen would get a hair up her ass, and the two of them would be spending time together at some point again, Jerry knew. The time had simply come, and it was, as Vivian had reminded him, probably better for Luke to get to know his mother than to feel abandoned and unloved for the rest of his life. Jerry decided to pull himself together and make the most of this night with his sweet wife. "Did you get dessert?" he asked as he stood to face her.

"I got you a cream horn from the bakery," she said.

"God, I love you." He gave her a kiss on the forehead and a pat on the butt before heading for the bedroom in the back of the house. "Give me ten minutes to clean up and we'll eat," he yelled over his shoulder as he hobbled down the hallway.

And just like that, he realized he was hobbling. He'd have to take a look at the wound in his leg, which was now making the entire bottom half of his leg throb. He limped his way to the bed and pulled his shoes off before lifting the leg of his jeans to reveal the ugly red lump with two puncture wounds in the middle. The area felt warm to the touch, and streaks of pain radiated away from the area. Jerry knew that was not a good sign. *What the hell is going on?* he thought to himself. At that moment, a movement beside him startled him and he jerked backward on the bed. He had seen a dark flash that seemed to cross over his feet, running from left to right and ending near the open doorway. But now—there was nothing there. And then, another flash of shadow movement hovered in the doorway for a second before flashing back up the hallway, toward the living room—and toward his wife. *What in the holy hell,* he thought. *I am losing my mind.*

Jerry grabbed a shoe and ran up the hallway with it held over his head. He was acting on instinct, not yet realizing how bizarre it might look to Vivian, whom he ran past while holding the shoe in a threatening clutch.

He froze after he past her, and he felt her stare.

"Do we have mice?" he asked.

"I— don't think so." Vivian's face registered somewhere between shock and amusement. "Did you see something?"

"I'm not sure. I mean, I think I did." Jerry knew he was sounding insane, but he couldn't really sort crazy thoughts from rational ones at the moment. He looked around the living room, where he now stood, and searched for any sign of movement. There was nothing.

"I'll call someone in to take a look," Vivian said. "But I really doubt it. Mice don't invade until fall, when the weather turns." She was laughing a little as she spoke. "Now go get yourself ready for dinner. I'm starving."

"Okay," Jerry said, realizing his voice sounded like that of a small child. This was bewilderment, he realized. He had never felt it before, but he was totally bewildered at the events of the past few days, and he had no idea what was happening. Maybe it was his mind, some residue from the hypnotic experience during the conference that was making him hallucinate now.

Josh would know. Josh was a psychologist. He'd call Josh tomorrow and tell him everything, and Josh would have an answer. But for now, he needed to find some pain killers.

## 6

## DATA FABRICATION

"I have to be honest with you, man, that's just not something I know much about."

Jerry closed his eyes, slumped forward on the couch seat, and let his phone slip down below his ear in frustration. This wasn't the sort of response he'd hoped to get from Josh. He desperately needed to find out what the hell was going on in his life, but Josh apparently wasn't capable of shedding any light on the situation. And so far, Jerry had only told him that he was seeing flashes of shadows; there was no way he was ready to open up about the wound in his leg, which was getting worse by the hour. "Well," Jerry said, "Do you know of an expert on the power of suggestion or something? I mean, it has to be something like that going on."

"Actually, the power of suggestion is a something a little different. Suggestion can be used to modify how you behave or respond, but it isn't something that would make you hallucinate, as far as I know. *Hypnotic* suggestion, maybe. Can I talk to a guy I know and get back to you?"

"That would be great," Jerry said. At least it was something.

"So, you're going forward with our project? I mean, it sounds like you're onto something. If you figure out what's going on with you, with the visions and all, then you have some good stuff to say when we present our results next year. I'm really getting excited about this idea."

"Oh, you'd better believe it," Jerry said. "I am going to nail the bastard who is messing with my brain. I'll mention him by name." Actually, the presentation project had been the farthest thing from Jerry's mind lately, but it was true: once he figured out what kind of shit the old man had played on him, Jerry was going to nail him with legal action.

"Sweet," Josh said. "I know David is going through with his end of the deal, too. I talked to him this morning. He's pretty smitten with that Bigfoot hunter. Can you freakin' believe that?"

Jerry was struggling to keep his mind from wandering off. The pain in his leg was worrying him. "Yeah, that's crazy."

"So I guess I'm off to study alien abductions, then. It's going to be a crazy summer!"

"Yeah, so can you get back to me about your hypno-suggestion thing?" Jerry needed to end the conversation soon. He hated to be so abrupt with Josh, since he was asking for a favor and all, but he couldn't concentrate. He was relieved when Josh took the hint and ended the conversation. He had a feeling it was time to take a close look at his leg again. He lifted his foot and let it rest on the coffee table and began the gentle task of rolling up his pant leg. Just as he'd expected, the red area around the puncture was growing. Jerry could feel the pain deep into his muscle and up his entire leg.

"What the hell happened to you!"

He had no idea how long Vivian had been standing there, just a few feet beside him, and the shrillness in her voice was both startling and unnerving. He'd been trying to convince himself that the little wound on his leg would heal itself, but it was starting to hurt like holy hell. It was also looking pretty ugly to Jerry, and by the sound of her voice, Viv thought so, as well.

"You need to have that looked at! How did that happen?"

Vivian's words were coming so quickly that Jerry didn't have time to make up a good lie. "I was in a parking lot and fell," he said.

"What do you mean? How did you fall?" Her rapid fire questions made him feel like a guilty school boy.

"I don't know. I just fell on something."

"Fell on *what*?"

"I don't know what! It was dark!"

"Oh, whatever," she said, sounding a bit impatient with his vagueness. "Get up. I'm taking you to the ER right now. I think it's getting infected."

Jerry knew not to put up any resistance, and he was a little relieved to have his wife take charge, as she tended to do in tense situations. His mind was trying to stay in denial about the whole thing, since the wound had happened in such an inexplicable way. He had to agree that medical attention was the most pressing issue at the moment.

"HOW LONG AGO DID THIS HAPPEN?" The emergency room doctor squinted his eyes and gripped Jerry's leg with both hands before rotating it toward the light for a better view.

His grip made the pain shoot up into Jerry's thigh. Jerry felt sweat dripping down his back.

"Day before yesterday." He couldn't help wincing as he spoke.

"Can you be more specific?" the doctor said. "How many hours?"

"About forty-eight."

"I know you said you fell," the man said. "Did you see what you fell on?" The look on his face was concerning.

"Uh, not really," Jerry said. "And I guess it was a little less than forty-eight hours, now that I think about it." He needed to be precise about the timing, since he was so clueless about the nature of the wound. "Late afternoon."

"You say you've had a tetanus shot recently?"

"A year ago."

"I want you to think, then," the doctor said. "Is there any chance there was a snake where you fell?"

*A snake?* In all honesty, the punctures could have come from anything, since Jerry had been hallucinating at the time it occurred. Would that man have been crazy enough to allow a venomous snake attack an audience member? This wasn't making any sense at all. Jerry was now feeling nauseous, and the sickness interfered with his ability to think straight. "Honestly, doctor, there could have been. I really have no idea."

"You were in Savannah, right? Near a river?"

"Yeah," Jerry said.

"No way to be sure," the man said, still attempting to rotate Jerry's leg, "It's not acting like a simple puncture; I believe there's some kind of toxin at work here. If I had to make a guess, I'd say copperhead. Your symptoms are some-what consistent with copperhead venom, although the the reactions are slower than I'd expect. It's weird, but definitely not anything more venomous. Any other snake bite would have killed you by now."

"Reassuring," Jerry said as he glanced at Vivian with a *what the hell* look. "So do I need some kind of antivenin?"

"Not an option at this point," the doctor said. "But we do need to keep you here for observation. I'll find you a room."

The doctor swooped out of the room in the usual abrupt, doctorly style. Jerry wasn't sure if it was the smell of the hospital or the insane circumstances he was dealing with, but he was starting to feel strange—like woozy and emotional all at once. To make matters worse, he'd hardly slept the night before because he was worried that his son was having too much fun at his born-again mother's house and would get ideas about living with her. Thankfully, Viv was there with him. He gave her his most loving glance.

"Why the hell did you lie to me?" she said in return.

"What?" Jerry said defensively. "When did I lie?"

"You told me it was dark out and you stumbled. You just told the doctor that it was about forty-eight ago, and this—whatever it is—happened to you in the middle of the day. Jerry, what in the hell are you up to?"

Her heartless tone was more than he could handle. He never was good at juggling lies, and his emotions were now flooding to the surface and causing his eyes and nose to flow freely. He was starting to cry.

"What the *hell*?" Gerald James Price, you need to tell me what is going on, right now."

"Vivian," he said in an unintentional whisper. His throat was so tight that his voice was quiet and quivering. "I do have something to tell you, but I can't go into it right now. Can we talk after we get home?"

"Are you having an affair?"

The absurdity of her accusation snapped him out of his

weepy fog. "That is absurd," he said as he laughed through the tears. "You really are an idiot."

"Well, you're an idiot, too. Why are you keeping something from me?"

Jerry looked back at his wife, whom he loved more than anything on earth, except for the son they'd raised together. How was he going to explain to her that he was losing his mind? She'd stayed by his side through all the bullshit caused by his crazy ex, through the starving years he'd caused as a struggling student and as an assistant professor in the history department. While they'd faced a lot of challenges together, this situation might be the one to take them down. He couldn't see how he could tell Vivian the truth, but he also knew he couldn't keep things from her. He was afraid. "Vivian," he said, although that wasn't the word that actually came out of his mouth. It was more like a a *fluuvr-rrren* sound that he made, and for the life of him, he couldn't understand why his lips hadn't moved like they should. He saw a frightened look on Vivian's face, just before he heard a loud noise and felt a sharp pain in his temple. He was pretty sure it was the sound of his head hitting the floor. And that was all he knew before everything went black.

## 7

## PARADIGM SHIFT

"We still have to have that talk," Vivian said, as she settled a tray of food on Jerry's lap. "I've been easy on you while you were in the hospital, but I do expect an explanation. I need to know what the hell is going on."

"I know," Jerry said with a sigh. He'd known this was coming, but after two days in the hospital, he wasn't any more sure about what he would say. He fluffed a pillow and threw it behind him to prop himself more upright on the bed and adjusted his hips. It was clear to both of them that he was stalling.

"Well, you can calm yourself for now," she said, as she patted his knee. "I think there's something more pressing you need to deal with at the moment." She moved around the bed to sit next to him. Now she was the one stalling and he was the one wrinkling his forehead in concern. Her face was taught with worry. "It's Luke, honey. Something's not right."

"Oh, my god," Jerry said. "Don't tell me. He's been spending time with his mother while I was in the hospital. I knew it."

"Right," Vivian said. "He has. But that's not the problem. I mean, I'm sure that's at the bottom of it somehow, but that's not what I wanted to tell you."

*"What?"* Jerry nearly yelled the word. "Tell me what's wrong!"

Vivian squeezed his knee as she looked toward the door, signaling that she wanted Jerry to quiet down. At the moment, Luke was in his own bedroom across the hall with the door shut.

"Has he come out of his room to talk to you at all since you've been home?" she asked.

"No," Jerry said. "I figured he feels weird because I gave him a scare or something. We haven't really talked."

"That's the thing," Vivian said. "He stopped talking to his mom, and she blames me for it. However, he won't talk to me, either. And now he hasn't even spoken to you, after everything. I don't know what's going on."

"Get him in here." Jerry felt that awful panic that only a parent can feel. It wasn't like Luke to stop communicating, and Jerry knew something bad was at the bottom of this.

"Don't be hard on him—"

"Go get him, Vivian," Jerry interrupted. His head was swirling with all sorts of bad scenarios. Luke had always been a great kid, and Jerry knew he was damned lucky for that. He lived in fear, though, of drugs, or girls, or some bully punk, or some sick weirdo getting in his head and screwing up his brain. "I want to get to the bottom of it, *now*." He felt a little bad for speaking to Vivian more harshly than he'd intended, but his heart was thumping with fear for his kid, and whatever this was, it was happening on top of the fact that his leg was burning with a wound from some imaginary fiend. *How the hell much was he supposed to take?*

Vivian left and crossed the hall to summon Luke from

the self-imposed isolation of his room, and Jerry could tell that his son tried to hesitate at first. Vivian showed an aggression that was unusual for her, pounding and raising her voice, until the dazed face of their son emerged from behind the door. "Go see your father, now," she said. Jerry couldn't remember Vivian using such a stern voice on Luke, mostly because it had never been necessary. *Jesus*, he thought. His whole house was suddenly in turmoil.

When Luke walked into the room, Jerry's heart felt like hot lead, all balled up inside his chest. The boy's eyes were sunken, and he seemed more pale than he'd ever been. "Come over here, son," Jerry said. "Give your dad a hug." Jerry could hear his own heart beating. He didn't know what he was about to learn, and he didn't know if he was going to be able to handle it. Luke approached the bed and reached out his arms, and as soon as he got within arm's reach of Jerry, tears started streaming down his face. Jerry grabbed his son by the shoulders and looked into his eyes. "Hey, man. You're scaring me now. Sit down here and tell me what's going on." Jerry was terrified.

"I can't," Luke said.

"You're gonna," Jerry said. "You're not leaving this room until you tell me what's bugging you." He tried hard to keep his voice steady. Whatever was wrong, Jerry didn't want to make it worse by letting his emotions show too much. "Is it your mom?" Jerry asked. "Do you want to go live with her? Are you afraid I'll be mad?" This was just one of the scenarios popping up in Jerry's brain.

"No," Luke said meekly.

Jerry's chest thumped harder, and he realized that the awful scenario he'd just mentioned had been the least of his fears. So whatever the thing was, it was worse than that.

"I can't tell you," Luke said. He sniffled and wiped tears from his nose with his palm.

"Listen, child," Jerry said. His shaky voice was betraying him, now. The panic was evident. "You're going to tell me, I don't care what it is." He was nearing hysteria. He'd rarely used this tone with Luke, and it was breaking his heart.

"But you won't believe me!" This time Luke was yelling. "Nobody will believe me."

"Of course I'll believe you," Jerry shouted back. "We don't lie to each other, remember?"

"You'll say I'm crazy," Luke said. He was starting to sob, now. "I don't want to tell you because I know you won't believe me."

For a moment, a thought flashed through Jerry's brain that was so outlandish that he dismissed it as wishful thinking. But his son had said the same words Jerry had been thinking for days. *Nobody will believe me.*

"Son," Jerry said, but this time he was whispering. "Did you see something weird? I mean, *really* weird?"

Luke looked back at his father with a mix of shock and hopefulness on his face. "What do you mean?" he asked.

"I'm asking you. Did you see something weird that makes you think you're hallucinating?"

Luke stared back, apparently stunned speechless, with a bright pink face and watery eyelashes. "How did you know that?" he whispered.

In a sudden rush, Jerry felt every truth he had ever believed drain from his soul. He couldn't believe that he was considering the impossible, but even the impossible would be preferable to seeing his kid suffer from drugs or abuse, like he'd prepared himself for. He reached over and jerked a tissue from the box on the bedside table. "Tell me son," he said in a calm, matter of fact voice. "What did it look like?"

His son continued to stare back at him with wide open eyes and mouth.

"Was it some weird little shadow creature lurking in a corner or streaking up and down the hallway?" Jerry continued. He knew he sounded like a madman, but he could tell from his son's reaction that the insane, impossible scenario he was suggesting was about to be confirmed. He was almost laughing, now, as he tossed a tissue at his stunned child. "Was that it?" he yelled.

"Yes!" Luke shouted back to his father, but this time he was laughing and crying, all at once. "Yes," he repeated, in some wild hysteria through his tear-swollen face. "How did you know that, dad?"

Jerry grabbed his son and pulled him in for a tight hug. Now he was also talking through tears. He was crying in an odd sort of relief. "It's okay, son. It's going to be okay. I guess we've got a fucking troll in the house—or something." Jerry squeezed the boy tighter than he ever had before, and they both laugh-cried like a pair of maniacs.

## 8

## PEER REVIEW

David punched at a pillow behind his head and adjusted himself on the bed before picking up the TV remote and hitting the play button with his thumb. He turned the volume down low, fearing that one of his neighbors on either side might hear that he was watching a Sasquatch show. He lived in a nice condo unit, but he had noticed that noise from his neighbor's TV had penetrated the walls occasionally, especially late at night. There were faculty members living on each side of him, so there was no way he wanted them overhearing this.

The intro to the show was just as Jerry had described it; a distinguished sounding announcer was itemizing a long list of Laura London's scholarly credentials, while "Wild Thing" played in the background. It was one of David's favorite songs, in fact. That, alone, impressed him. It hit him again, what a big deal she was in some circles. The thought of thousands of people tuning in to watch this woman was thrilling, and a little odd. Their conversations had turned flirty right away, and the two of them seemed to have rare chemistry. It was such foreign territory for him. He hadn't felt this way for so many years, he couldn't even count them.

He lifted a beer to his lips and sipped as the show began. There was Laura, apparently deep in the woods of Pennsylvania, with a lone cameraman named Chaz tagging along—at least that was the claim. David suspected there were others joining in, off camera. For several minutes, he watched while Laura and Chaz sat in the dark, listening to sounds of crickets and twig snaps as the camera swung around them, and Laura narrated stories of recent sightings in the area. This went on for five minutes or so, and David was just about to fast forward when the sound of a larger *crack* caused an exchange of excited whispers between Laura and the cameraman.

*This had better start getting interesting*, David thought. The show was about to lose him.

The screen now showed the image of dark tree-like shapes with a few hulky, green-glowing lumps on the edges. This, Laura explained, was the night vision image of something lurking behind a tree about twenty yards away from them.

David leaned in to look closer at his screen, when one lump turned into two lumps.

"There are two!" Laura whispered excitedly on the screen.

At that moment, the green lumps extended into two gigantically tall lumps, which appeared to turn around and bound away into the thickness of the forest. Laura's voice estimated the taller one to be about nine feet in height.

"I can't believe people buy this," David said softly to himself. He was feeling a little sick to his stomach, now. He was so damned confused. Was he, of all people, about to get involved with a circus performer? A small lump was forming in his throat. But then—maybe she was actually a victim of trickery, herself? It was still possible that the show's producers had manufactured this chicanery without her knowing. He fast forwarded and landed about three quarters of the way through the show before resuming play. This was the part of the show where Laura interviewed people who had supposedly experienced some sort of traumatic encounter. As the action started again, David was surprised to see that Laura was sitting face to face with a young boy. He let out a loud sigh and placed the remote control on the bed beside him and crossed his arms. As painful as this might be for David, he needed to watch this. If the woman of his dreams would sink low enough to exploit the imagination of a young boy for ratings, David had to know.

The boy was from a nearby Ohio county, not far from David's home town, and he had big hazel eyes and a head of moppy brown hair that hung down beneath a Cleveland Browns hat. His name was Sawyer. David noticed that Laura held on to Sawyer's hand as they made their introductions and chatted for a few minutes. Then she started to gently question the child, who explained that he lived on a farm with his parents and his little brother, who was only three. Sawyer's bedroom was on the second floor of their house, he explained, and on the night of his experience, he was trying to go to sleep, but he couldn't, because his dad's hunting dogs were making a lot of noise.

"So what did you do?" Laura asked. "Did you get out of bed?"

"No," the boy said. "I didn't have to. I can see out the window from my bed. I just got up on my knees and looked out."

"Do you want to tell us what you saw?"

"Okay," Sawyer said. He looked at his mother, who was beside him on a short couch, and she nodded back in encouragement. "I saw a big spider," he said. "First I saw one, and then I saw another one. They were in front of the dog pens."

"Oh?" Laura seemed a little surprised, but composed herself quickly. "I see. That must have been really scary."

David was confused. He thought the boy was about to claim he saw a giant hairy man, so he had no idea what kind of story he was hearing now.

"What did you do?" Laura asked.

"I ran into my mom and dad's room to tell them I saw a giant spider, but my dad didn't understand. He said it was just a spider, and I should go to sleep."

"I feel so bad," the boy's mother whispered. "We thought he was freaking out about a big spider on his wall. It's a farmhouse. We get those a lot."

"It wasn't a spider in my room, though!" Sawyer insisted. "It was outside, and it was giant. Like, it was as big as a car. It was really creepy."

"I know it was giant," Laura said as she squeezed his hand. "I know lots of people who've seen what you saw. They weren't really spiders, though," Laura added. "You know that, right?"

"That's what my mom told me," he said in his little boy voice. He hesitated before starting again. "She said they were Sasquatches. She says that sometimes they can crawl on their bellies and put their knees and elbows up like this to sneak up on things." As he spoke, he twisted his arms around to jut his elbows skyward. "It makes them look a lot like giant, hairy spiders. Especially when it's dark out."

"I learned that on your show," the mom said.

"That is absolutely right," Laura said. "That seems to be

how they crawl sometimes, when they are trying to make sure they stay out of sight."

"And you believe me?" Sawyer asked. "That I saw them?"

"I sure do," Laura said. The boy smiled at his mother and looked back at Laura. "A lot of people watching this show believe you, too. You don't have to feel alone."

"They got one of daddy's dogs," he said. "One of them was missing in the morning."

Laura's mouth fell open, but she composed herself quickly. "I'm really sorry about that," she said.

"It's okay," the boy shrugged. "I feel real bad for the dog, but I wasn't allowed to play with them or anything. They were hunting dogs. And they can run really fast. I think maybe it got away from the spider. I mean the Sasquatch."

"I'll bet it did get away," Laura smiled. She patted the boy on his hand.

"Okay," Sawyer said, as if to signal he was done talking.

David watched as Laura continued to comfort both mother and child, and advised them both to call her personal phone if they had any more trouble with the creatures. She assured them that this encounter was most likely a one-time event, and that the creatures were probably on the move, since they didn't usually stay in one place too long. Even though the words that came from her mouth sounded like crazy talk to David, he was impressed with her kindness.

Thoughts were racing through his head. He'd never felt inner turmoil like this before, and frankly, he couldn't think of a way out of this strange situation. Should he keep up the charade, and spend the summer pretending like he was okay with her bizarre work and beliefs?

On the other hand, and David couldn't believe he was actually entertaining this thought, was there some real situation out there that made these people believe what they did? Not that he believed that there was a large, undiscovered humanoid lurking in the woods, but it was possible that something real was giving that impression. For instance, maybe it was possible that bears were the real culprits. Maybe there was some unknown disease that made bears behave strangely, and that this was the reason people believed the way they do?

David realized that the show had ended, and he was staring blankly at the screen, so he picked up his phone and tapped "mistaken for a Sasquatch" in the search bar. He was comforted to find, as he scrolled down the page, that it was quite common for bears to be confused for unknown animals. The act of walking upright was not as uncommon as once believed, and it was quite common for people to be fooled by this and other behaviors that were not common knowledge. He tossed the phone down again, but the sound of a *ping* made him look back once more. He could see that he'd received a text from Laura.

"Did you watch it? What did you think?"

She knew he'd intended to watch the recording. She seemed to genuinely care how he felt about it. He wasn't sure how to answer her, since he wasn't at all sure how the hell he felt about the show or the entire phenomenon. But there was one thing that was crystal clear. The sound of the ping, and the realization that Laura London was on the other end of it, had caused his heart to race like nothing in the world had ever done before. He couldn't back out of this whole arrangement, now. However things turned out, he just couldn't quit right now. His curious nature just wouldn't permit it. But more to the point, and to David's genuine surprise, his own heart wouldn't allow it.

## 9

## LITERATURE REVIEW

David lifted a wine glass to his lips and shifted his eyes from table to table around the restaurant. "I'm not used to people staring at me while I eat."

Across the table, Laura flashed a quick, sassy smile and reached across to pat his free hand. "They're not looking at you, honey."

It was unbelievable to him, how much the simple feel of her touch sent tiny needle pricks shimmering up his arm to make his face flush. This was the first time he'd ever considered that the term chemistry, when applied to two people, could prompt a real physical reaction. He'd been in plenty of relationships before, and with some very attractive women, but he'd never experienced a palpable reaction from a simple glance or touch. There was something different about her beauty. While there was perfection in her flawless skin and her long, brown ringlets of hair that bounced as she walked, the beauty of this woman rested like a cloud in and around her. Being near her was beautiful.

"Very funny," he stuttered, trying to sound as calm as she was. "And *some* of them are looking at me." From his view behind the glass, David could spot at least four sets of eyes gazing straight toward his table. "They're wondering why the beautiful, kooky monster hunter is hanging out with such an ugly dude. But seriously, does this happen everywhere?"

"Most places," Laura said. "But you get used to it. People tend to leave you alone until you finish your meal, then one or two may wander over to say hello or ask for an autograph. I just try not to make eye contact, because that's usually interpreted as an invitation. And for the record, your ugliness is only in the inside."

"You do wonders for my ego," David said. He settled his glass on the table and tried to keep his eyes from darting outside the sphere of their dinner table, but it was futile. He could feel the stares boring into the side of his head, and he couldn't keep from glancing sideways.

It was all so strange, spending time with this woman. In addition to her mind-numbing beauty, her apparent fame was a constant, unavoidable factor to deal with. They couldn't be in public alone, and while it was part of the woman's appeal, it was also odd and somewhat annoying.

Like most people, David had dreamed of being famous when he was younger. He had the good looks at the time, with his tall physique and dark features. At the age of fifteen, he was pretty certain his guitar skills were going to propel him to rockstar fame, and he'd been sure his handsome face would afford him the sweet life of traveling, making a little music, and conquering thousands of adoring virgins. He wasn't sure exactly when he'd gone off the rails so much and decided to live the life of an academic, instead. Now he spent his days reading and grading papers. He'd been on the road to turning into a big, fat, distinguished but perpetually single professor, until this whole paranormal project came along. Now, here he was, suddenly, getting a taste of the celebrity life. He wasn't sure where this whole adventure was going to end up, but if he wasn't really careful, he could end up feeling like a real heel. And maybe a heartbroken one. After all, his main goal this summer was to find a way to discredit this woman, along with her life's work. He was starting to realize that this wasn't going to be easy. As nutty as this girl was, he really liked her. She made him laugh, she made him think, and recently, she'd made him get his body in better shape. She'd traveled to join him in his own small, Ohio town for a few weeks, in an effort to prepare him for the ordeal he'd signed up for. For one thing, he'd have to work out every day in preparation for their summer hikes together. "You'll need to be in top shape to keep up with me all summer," she'd said about their pending series of hikes through some remote forests. The locations of these adventures, he couldn't say just yet. She had promised to fill him in on a need to know basis, since discretion was required by her contract with the TV network.

"Earth to David," Laura said from across the table. "Where did you go?"

"I was just wondering where you're taking me next week," he said. "Am I allowed to know the state?"

"No." she said. He loved the way her brown eyes flashed when she was mean to him. "Or maybe after dessert," she teased.

David just sighed and shook his head in response. He couldn't really object too much. After all, he wasn't exactly behaving like a choir boy. She was right not to trust him.

"I have a present for you," she said, as she reached around to pull a small bundle from her handbag. The look on his face must have revealed the momentary panic he felt.

"Don't worry," she said. "It's not a real gift; it's more like an assignment."

He took the package from her hand and could tell from the feel of it that it contained a paperback book. As he tore away the paper, he revealed a professional photo of Laura, smiling from the back cover. He turned it over to reveal the title, *Bigfoot: Arguments and Answers.*

"Yours?" he said, maneuvering his face in a desperate attempt to look enthusiastic. Just a few weeks ago, the thought of owning a book on this topic would have been absurd. Actually, it still was preposterous to him, and he was trying mightily not to show it.

"You look like you're going to throw up," she giggled. So much for hiding his feelings.

"I'm just—surprised."

"You are horrified." Again, she was able to see right through his facade. "But you're *going* to read it," she continued. "If you're going to do this with me, I need you to understand how serious this topic is. Or, at least, I need to start chipping away at that big wall of negativity. I know it's hard for you. I've met a lot of people like you. But here's the thing: most of them have had a change of heart." She punctuated her statement with a seductive wink.

"I—uh," he stammered. He felt as if his brain and his heart were at war, and his brain was clearly losing the battle. He couldn't conjure any words that were comfortable coming out of his lips. He could either insult her now, and end this wonderful adventure, or he could tell a big lie that she'd see right through. His mind was paralyzed.

"Relax," she said. "Just set it aside for now."

She was trying to be merciful, he could tell, but he'd been pushed into a place he was hoping to avoid for as long as he could. He'd never felt such internal conflict, and there was no point in trying to avoid it every moment he was in her company. "I'm sorry," he finally managed. "This is really hard. I'm trying to keep an open mind—"

"No, you are not."

Her response was abrupt, but not confrontational. She seemed genuinely amused.

"David," she laughed out his name. "I'm not stupid, remember? I know exactly how you're feeling. Just relax, I frankly don't care how you feel right now. I see you as my student."

"Well, that's awkward," he stammered. "The student part. It messes up a lot of my plans for this summer." He was glad to work his way back toward their normal flirtatious talk.

"Well, we both know taboos just make things more exciting." She lifted her eyebrows as she spoke, and her gesture made the blood drain from his torso. At that moment, a server approached their table and placed a sizzling ribeye in front of him. He wondered if he'd be able to choke down any part of it. Although he hadn't eaten since his breakfast cereal, food had lost all appeal to him.

"And listen, you can stop being all twisted up inside, afraid of saying things to offend me," she continued. "I am so confident that you'll change your tune by the end of this summer, that you can say anything you want. I'll just remain smug."

Her confidence made her seem crazy but sexy at the same time. But he did feel relieved that he didn't have to worry so much about offending her. The fine line he'd been trying to walk had widened by an inch or so, at least for now. As the summer wore on, his reality checks would wear down her patience at some point, he knew. But he could worry about that later. "So can I start with one question?" he asked.

"Of course. Anything you want."

"Why no bodies?" He'd decided to jump into the thick of the controversy to test her confidence. It was a risk, but he couldn't see any way around the situation. If he was ever going to be able to relax around this woman, he had to find out where her boundaries were placed, and how penetrable they truly were. He was all in now.

She placed her elbows on the table, placed her chin on her clasped hands, and sighed. "The long answer is in the book. That's why I gave it to you."

"No good," he said. "Give me a quick summary."

"Okay. There are bodies. There *have* been bodies."

David rocked back in his chair. "Oh, really? Why haven't I seen this on the news?"

"Read the book. Next question."

"Okay," he said. "So if there's so much proof and it's easy to find, why don't real anthropologists get involved?"

"They are involved." She plopped another bite into her mouth and gave him a smirk with one eyebrow raised in a reminder that she *was* an anthropologist. Awkward.

"DNA evidence?"

"It's readily available. People call it fake news."

David put both hands on his head in frustration. "So I get the feeling you want me to read the book?"

"Bingo. So now can I ask you one question? You have to promise to think about it and not be offended."

"Of course," he said.

"Why is it that scientists are the most closed-minded people of all?"

"That's absurd," he snapped. The very notion was offensive to him, a man who had dedicated his life to discovery and progress.

"Is it, really?" she asked.

The question bothered him more than he wanted to admit. He wasn't closed minded. Good scientists *can't* be. He realized he was now chewing his steak aggressively and slowed down a bit. He took a sip of wine and let it settle before speaking. "I'm not gullible," he said. "That's how I see it."

For the first time, he saw a flash of something like annoyance on her face, but she recovered quickly. "Great," she said. "So that means you'll be able to admit freely that you are wrong, when the evidence is in front of you."

"Definitely." He noticed that both of them were speaking in curt sentences. "Real evidence."

"Fair enough," she beamed a fake smile. "North Georgia."

"Huh?"

"That's where we're going next week."

"Ahhhh, so Sasquatch is there?" He smiled sheepishly, knowing he was pressing her buttons.

"Maybe, but we're not going there to see him." She was totally ignoring his playfulness now. So, she wasn't as bullet proof as she liked to pretend. "We're going to a campfire meeting. That's something that takes place once a year, when researchers and enthusiasts get together and discuss their recent findings and their plans for the upcoming summer. And I'm going in the hopes of charming a certain scientist from Ipswich University."

"Ipswich?" David asked, noting the surprise in his own voice. Despite its small size, the college had one of the best anthropology programs in Europe.

"Yes, dear. Ipswich." She had that annoyed look again. "This guy has been tracking several family groups for years. He's well funded and loaded with technology and resources, but he's pretty secretive about his findings. He doesn't have much time for doubters."

David's brain was stuck on the words "family groups." People actually believe there were clans of these creatures roaming the deep woods? The guy was apparently some self-proclaimed expert on Sasquatch social behavior. This was all so bizarre.

"However," she continued, "He knows about my show, and we've exchanged a few emails, so I'm hoping he makes an appearance. If I can get him to support an expedition, you are in for the ride of your life."

She was so beautiful, sitting there across from him, staring back across the table. Indeed, he was definitely in for the ride of his life, one way or another, and he had no idea how this would all end up.

"Then I'll buckle up tight," he said.

## 10

## MEETING OF MINDS

"This your first time out?"

David tried to pretend he hadn't heard the scrawny, wrinkly-skinned man who sat sweating through his T-shirt on the other end of a log. The man had shoulder length, white hair, and he sat with one leg wrapped around the other, like a sexy woman might do, only it looked really creepy on an old man. Of all the people gathered at this event—and there were hundreds from all over the world—this guy had decided to strike up a conversation with him. And he wasn't giving up easily. He poked David on the bare leg with a branch he'd described earlier as a snake stick. "Oy, chap," the man said in a pompous English tone.

"Excuse me?" David said, not really trying to hide his annoyance. The man just smiled back with a wide grin. He was peering from under a white, wide-brimmed hat that made David want to swat the priggish little weirdo off the far end of the log.

"I thought so," the man said. "You're not a believer, are you?"

"I'm here with a friend." David said, crossing his arms

and outstretched legs and trying to imply that the conversation was over. He was holding out hope that the man would go away and commune with the other storytellers gathered around the fire, but he suspected it was no use. This guy seemed to be the leechy type.

"Oh, yes!" he said. "You're Miss London's friend." The man bit a long shred of wood from one end of his snake stick and rolled it in his mouth like a cigar. "I'm quite impressed by her work, I must say." He spoke from the free side of his mouth and couldn't have sounded more obnoxious if he'd tried. "And her *story*. Quite traumatizing, I would say, encountering the beast at such a young age as she did. She lost her horse, as I recall."

"Uh huh," David said, trying to sound as indifferent to the man as possible.

"Do you not believe her?"

This guy was really starting to piss him off, and David wanted desperately to punch his face. Was this guy really planning to defend Laura to *him*? He seemed like a creepy loser with no life; just the type he'd expect to find in a group like this. But then again, he had to remember that Laura was famous, and lots of people liked to claim her as an acquaintance. He glanced around until he locked eyes on Laura, who looked back at him from the far side of the campfire, seeming to sense his stare. As she gazed back at him, he did a quick eye roll to signal his disdain for his current company, but she didn't giggle back as he'd expected. Instead, she turned white and flashed a look of quick panic. She jumped to her feet and headed his way, as the man beside him droned on about how proud he was of Laura. It seemed like it took hours for her to make her way across the camp to get to his defense, and the old man went on and on.

"So you two have met?" Laura blurted once she reached

them. She seemed out of breath, and David could sense her anxiety. "David, I told you about Dr. Whythe, remember?" She was nearly frantic. "On the plane?" Her eyes were drilling holes in David's face. "From Ipswich?"

*Jesus Christ*, he thought. He should have known. "I'm honored," David lied. He tried his best to sound genuine for Laura's sake. "I didn't realize I was speaking with the professor, himself."

"No need to bullshit me, young man," the man said behind that broad, annoying grin. "You think I'm crazy as hell, don't you?"

In the fire glow, Laura's face suddenly resembled Munch's *The Scream*. "David!" she gasped in a distinct accusatory tone. "What have you said to him?"

"I don't, and I didn't," David said to both of them, glancing back and forth. "I mean, I'm not here to judge."

He wasn't even convincing himself.

"Really?" the old man said, still sucking on his imaginary cigar. "Then what, exactly, are you here to do?"

The bastard. He just sat there grinning across the awkward silence he'd just created. He was trying to force David to admit his true objective, right in front of Laura. Clearly, she knew he was skeptical about her beliefs, but he'd never come out and told Laura outright that his true mission was to actually disprove what she—and everyone else attending this crazy bonfire party—so fervently believed. But it seemed the old man could sense it.

"Observe," David answered. He regretted the word as soon as it came from his mouth.

"Really?" The old man was feigning confusion. "But, if you're not a believer, then what, or *whom*, exactly, do you hope to observe?" He glanced at Laura and back at David. The implication was evident.

David longed for the days back in the old neighborhood when he could punch a guy in the nose without much of a consequence. He'd punched a bully once back at school, and everyone cheered him for it. Why couldn't grownups be more like kids? Why couldn't they punch people who really deserved it? At the moment, this old bastard was really pissing him off. The old codger knew exactly what he was doing, implying that David was only along to charm his way into Laura's sleeping bag. Of course, it was true. He certainly wanted to get to that point, eventually. And Laura wasn't stupid; she had to know he was interested in her in a physical way, but they had an understanding. They planned to take things a day at a time and enjoy each other's company for now. But now, because of this jerk, Laura looked like she wanted to cry. David knew he couldn't win if he went up against her hero, even though he really wanted to send him ass over elbows down the nearest cliff. He took a deep breath.

"Listen. I am a man of science, just like you. I'm sure there was a time when you felt pretty much the same way I do. I'm trying to keep an open mind, but I need to see things for myself before I form any theories, alright? That's all."

"Well, that is interesting," the man said. "You see, when I came here, I fully intended to provide our friend Laura with some very special information." He turned to smile at her like a grandfather would a granddaughter, a smile with a long, adoring pause. "Information about a very active location where I'd like someone to go and research. You see, I'm not able to rough it in the wilderness like I used to. But I am a little concerned, now."

"Concerned about what?" Laura sounded excited and desperate at the same time. She glanced at David like he was a flea she was about to flick and sat on the log next to her hero. The bastard grabbed her hand.

"I'm sure it's obvious, my dear. This is serious business, as you know."

Laura looked up at David. "Can you excuse us? Just give us a few minutes, please?"

David clamped his lips together briefly before mustering an "Of course." He turned to leave the two of them alone to discuss just how disposable he was, and determine whether he was worthy of a good Sasquatch secret. Of all the ridiculous things he'd done for sex, this had to be the topper. At least he'd have a good, albeit short, story to tell the others if he was kicked out of the club on the first night. Jerry would never let him live this down. At this point, there was only one thing that could salve his broken ego, and that was a burning glob of sugary marshmallow. He headed for the fire pit area and snooped around for a marshmallow bag and a good stick, and found both with ease. He settled into a chair next to a lumberjack-looking guy, full beard and all.

"So where are we?" David asked.

"Whatcha mean?" the guy answered, looking perplexed.

"Well, I got off a plane in Atlanta and then sat on a bus for a while, that's all I know," David laughed. "Where is this place?"

"We're in a town called Winder," the man chuckled back. "Actually, a state park right outside. This is our main meeting place. We gather here every year, then we agree on assignments and go off to research in different places. You new?"

"Indeed," David said. "I'm a newbie." The guy squinted back in suspicion. David decided he wasn't very good at hiding his sarcasm. He also decided to try to control himself better this time, partly because he could see Laura and the old professor across the fire, engaged in animated discussion, and he felt his time here was short. "So what got you interested in this field?"

The man squirmed a bit in his chair. "Got the shit scared out of me once."

"Really?"

"Really. What about you?" This man was not exactly a talker. David was determined to pull a story out of him, though.

"To be honest, I'm curious," David said. "I'd like to hear what happened, if you don't mind. What happened? I mean, you look like an outdoorsy dude. What scared you?" He really was a bit curious. Plus, he needed to have some kind of story to tell afterward. This might be his only chance.

"Name's Kenny." The man held out a hand for David to shake. David was reminded that he was in the South, where it's uncouth to go diving into conversations without a proper introduction. It was a charming trait.

"David. Good to meet you."

"Well, be careful what you ask for, David," the man said. He stared at the crackling fire for a few seconds before resuming. "I was out huntin' with my dad a few years back, like we'd done for ten years in the exact same spot." Kenny removed his hat briefly to scratch his curly blond locks with a bent pinky finger. "I was sitting there in a deer stand and my dad was about a mile away in his. I thought I heard somebody walkin' up behind me, so I turned around all ticked off, since we had a huntin' lease there and there shouldn't be anybody stomping around. And there it was. I like 'ta died, right then and there."

David waited for the man to continue, but he just stared into the fire. "What did you see?"

"It was a monster," Kenny said, his voice more quiet than

before. "It was nothing other than a monster. If you see one, you'll know what I mean."

"Can you describe it?" David was enthralled. What could make this man so certain that he'd seen some creature instead of a bear, or a man in a ghillie suit? From his brief look into this phenomenon, he'd realized that this common hunting get-up was behind most so-called encounters.

Kenny put his head back and closed his eyes. "I hate to picture it, to be honest," he said. "Still gives me the willies." He continued after a quiet pause. "He looked kind of human, but he was twice as tall as any man, and he had shoulders about four feet wide. You really can't picture that until you see it in real life. It's like lookin' at the biggest bull you've ever seen, all muscle, covered with a little hair and standing upright. That's how massive they are. His waist was small, but he was like a giant body builder on steroids. His eyes was mean looking, like he was mad as hell and ready to kill me. His face was very expressive, just like a man's."

"How are you sure it wasn't a man?" David asked. It still sounded like a man in a ghillie suit.

"Well, I was sitting in a chair in a tree stand ten foot off the ground. The thing was looking me right in the eyes."

"Wow!" David said. He doubted the veracity of the man's claim, since that would have put a creature at around twelve feet in height. "So, what happened next? I mean, you saw it and then what did you do?"

"Well, I pissed myself."

David burst out a laugh and then tried to shut it down immediately, when he saw the look on Kenny's face. "I'm sorry," David said. "I just wasn't expecting that."

"It's alright," Kenny said. "I wasn't expecting that, neither. But that's what happens when you look face to face with a monster. I'm tellin' you what, I was sittin' there with a loaded gun by my side, but when that thing came walking up, it never even crossed my mind to use it. I just froze there and pissed all over myself and the creature just snorted up at the air a while. I reckon he was smelling me. He looked at me mean and grunted, and then he just walked away like he had all the time in the world. It took me a long time to go back out into the woods. I'm telling ya, be careful what you go lookin' for."

"But if it shook you up so much, why would you go out looking for one again?" David needed to understand what this guy was about. Like Laura, the man seemed to believe what he was saying. He actually seemed to be on the verge of tears when he gazed into the fire. And what person would admit to soiling himself in such a matter-of-fact way for giggles?

"Well," Kenny said in a slow drawl. "If you look into the face of something that isn't supposed to exist, you doubt your sanity for a long time. Then you start to try to figure out, one way or another, whether you're crazy or not crazy. You get kind of hooked."

"So, now you're trying to see one again, to prove you're not insane?"

"Nope. Already did that. I've had three sightings, now. Now I'm just hooked."

Before David could respond, he realized that Laura was standing next to his chair. The timing sucked. He actually wanted to press Kenny for more details: what color it was, what kind of facial features—that sort of thing. The guy seemed so genuine, but David couldn't exactly brush off Laura at the moment.

"We need to talk for a minute," Laura said as she patted his shoulder. "Excuse us," she said to Kenny.

Laura pulled him by the hand until they were well out of

earshot of the others who were scattered around the site. "I need you to listen," she said. "Don't talk."

David nodded in agreement.

"David, I really like you. I'd love to get to know you better."

*This was it*, he thought. *He was really getting jilted on the first night of his adventure.*

"Don't do this, Laura."

"You promised you wouldn't talk! Now, listen to me." She lifted a stern, threatening finger in front of his face. "This is my work. This is my life's passion. You are not going to fuck this up for me, so you have two choices. This man is sending me out to an incredible place. It's crazy with activity, he says. So here's the deal: you can go back home, and maybe we meet up at some other point, I don't know."

"Seriously?"

"Hush! I said two choices. We have lots of fun together. I don't know, we just click. So here it is: you can swear on everything that is holy that you will not interfere with my work, and you will support me while we're out there. Just support me and keep an open mind. Can you handle that?"

"Well, of course." He felt a little stunned, actually. He'd fully expected to be sent packing. "But what about him?" David pointed his thumb at the professor. "I figured he'd insist I leave."

"Not exactly," she said. "He actually wants you to go."

"To keep an eye on you out there. I get it."

"Well, yes. That, plus he says you'll poop your pants and cry like a baby when you have your first sighting. He kind of likes that idea."

## 11

## FIELD RESEARCH

Josh inched his car toward the ornate iron gate of Skylar Ranch—affectionally known as the famous alien ranch in some circles—and rolled down his window when he was within arm's reach of the call box. There were no instructions or markings on the metal device; only a small red button below what appeared to be a speaker. He pushed the button and hoped for a response. After several seconds, there was a crackle to indicate that somebody was paying attention on the other end. As he waited, he noticed a small camera perched on top of a tall post just inside the gate.

"Who is it?" a gruff voice finally rumbled from the box.

"Josh White. We spoke on the phone a few days ago?"

"The man from the college?" the voice answered. Josh wasn't at all surprised by the apparent scrutiny. His internet research revealed that the place was quite popular with thrill seekers and teenaged pranksters, and the rancher was menaced by daily visits from curious tourists and para-normal researchers hoping to get a look inside the place.

"Yes, sir. That's me," Josh said. He waved his hand in the

direction of the camera. After a few more seconds, he saw the metal gates vibrating and then moving slowly open and outward to reveal a long, dirt driveway. The path ahead of him stretched so far that Josh wondered if there was actually a house on the other end. As he slowly rolled the car through the gate, he could see a wide open landscape of yellow-brown grass punctuated by occasional trees and shrubs. In the background, rolling hills made an uneven skyline. The hills seemed to form a half circle in the faraway distance, cradling the valley and its contents. Josh rolled forward over the dirt drive until the burnt orange roof of a single story dwelling rose from the land and revealed bricks and windows beneath it. As the trees stretched further into the distance on the left, a large field appeared. It was bordered by a wire fence and occupied by several clusters of grazing cattle. Josh recognized the landscape; he had seen it before, along with several million other people around the world. It was the same field that had appeared in the video that had brought this ranch onto the worldwide stage and prompted a mix of panic, hysteria, and cries of fraud.

Josh wasn't sure what he'd find when he first started the search into the UFO phenomenon. In fact, he'd been shocked to discover the long list of credible scientists who'd spoken out in support of the topic of extraterrestrial life. But there was a distinct difference between believing in the possibility of life existing elsewhere in the universe, and believing that these life forms were creepy, bug-eyed beings who visited earth and kidnapped human beings for experimentation, and slaughtered unsuspecting cows.

As he approached the house, Josh could see a bearded man standing by the front door with his arms crossed in front of him and a very no-nonsense look on his face. Josh pulled to the end of the drive and walked over to the man, who appeared to be Mr. Skylar, himself.

"Professor White?" the rancher said as he held out a hand.

"Call me Josh, please. Nice to meet you." Josh squeezed the man's calloused hand and noticed a tight grip. Whatever else this man might be, he was no stranger to hard physical labor.

"Chester Skylar," the man said, referring to his own name. "Folks call me Chet. I hope you remembered your camping gear." It was a not so subtle way of informing Josh that the house, itself, was off limits. He had received permission to spend time investigating the activity of the place for free, but he had not received anything resembling a warm and fuzzy embrace. While select visitors were allowed on the site, the rancher had made it clear that he'd had his fill of strangers coming onto his property to experience the strange happenings, only to follow up with insulting reports intending to debunk the video. "All I ever wanted was real answers," he'd said to Josh. "You're welcome to come in and investigate all you want, as long as you report the truth after you leave here."

It was an easy deal for Josh to accept, although he felt a twinge of guilt, knowing he was only here, in truth, to determine what sort of chicanery or psychosis was at play.

"I'll show you the place," Skylar said as he gestured toward a golf cart. "Grab your things and I'll take you back. It's right back there near the fence line. There's a place for a fire pit, and there's a washroom of sorts in the big barn nearby. You can stay as many nights as you like, but I reckon you'll be wantin' to leave after a night or two."

"Why do you say that?" Josh asked, as he stuffed his bags into the back of the cart and slid into the passenger seat. He assumed the man was setting the stage for whatever pre-arranged frights were to come.

Chet put the cart into gear and gazed forward in a look of something between disgust and dismay. "Everybody comes in the same. They don't expect anything to happen. Then something happens and scares the shit out of them and they high tail it. Then, probably after they get made fun of, they talk about how it was all some staged prank I pulled on them. Like I got money to waste on that kind of shit. I'm losing livestock here. And money."

"Sorry, man." Josh felt real emotion coming from the man. He was a good actor, or he had some kind of mental issue.

"I'm bettin' you'll get your dose of it. It's been quiet around here for two weeks now, and we don't normally get more than two solid weeks of quiet."

"What can I expect?" It was perfectly possible that somebody else was setting up this poor guy, Josh thought. How hard would it be to fly a drone over his place with a bright light attached, or create one that looked like a saucer? As for slaughtering animals, somebody could be stealing the meat and setting it up to look like something unworldly going on. Josh was starting to think this guy could be a victim, himself. There was something raw and genuine in his demeanor.

"Don't be shocked if you wake up to find one of the little bastards in the tent with you," Chet said. "They come in my house."

This was not the response Josh had expected.

## 12

# SPECIES

It was his fourth night of camp living, and the heat of the campfire felt good on his face. Josh was surprised the temperature dipped so low here in the summer. He could swear it was in the mid-fifties, and he was glad of it. The clear sky, the feel of the fire, the gentle moos from the livestock grazing nearby—it all left him in a magical state of peace, unlike anything he'd felt in a while. In fact, it seemed like he hadn't felt good about anything much at all for a long time. Once he'd finally finished his PhD, he thought he'd be able to embrace life with a strong sense of accomplishment, at last. But then the panic of finding a teaching job set in. After a few months of no responses and some family pressure, his Aunt Crystal finally agreed to help him secure a spot on the faculty at her university. The condition for this was that nobody find out that they were related. It had been an arrangement that Josh had regretted often, but maybe not as much as Crystal did. She demonstrated her disappointment with him at every opportunity, both in private and in front of his peers. Her snarky attitude toward him was so bad that it had raised a few eyebrows at meetings. So the job had also left him experiencing a big case of imposter syndrome, a condition that was not all that unusual among professionals, but Josh knew he had a particularly crippling case of it. He never felt like he measured up to the professors around him and he always felt like the outsider. Even when he tried, Crystal would make her way into his office and hit him with, "You're slacking on your job," or "You're letting down your department." More than once, Josh had tried to find teaching jobs at smaller colleges, far away from his aunt's mockery and ridicule, but he just couldn't get a break. It's not like he spent a lot of time sulking and dwelling on his situation, but these days of serenity on the ranch just seemed to highlight how unhappy he'd been for a few years. Josh wondered to himself if it might be time to force some type of positive change. Or maybe that was crazy, sleepy talk. It was almost midnight, and he was feeling every hour of his long day weighing down his eyelids. It was time to make his bed and settle in for the night.

He glanced at the tents in the distance, and realized that his camp mates had already retired for the evening. There were two other visitors at the ranch when Josh had arrived. One was Randy, a retired truck driver, who claimed he'd seen enough weird shit in his years on the road to make him curious about paranormal stuff. He seemed like a nice, otherwise sensible guy with a great sense of humor. The other was, to Josh's slight amusement, a woman somewhere in her sixties. Her name was Melanie, and she had divorced well, which left her with enough money to do whatever she wanted with her life. She used part of that money to spend a few weeks every six months or so at Skylar Ranch, and she actually footed the bill for installing toilets and showers in the big barn. She had never had children, so the money she didn't spend on thrill seeking ventures went to her odd hobbies and charities. She described herself as an aging hippie, although she seemed remarkably fit for her age, and she was somewhat of a naturalist. Josh had learned a lot about edible plants and natural medicine in their brief discussions over beer. He liked both Randy and Melanie, and Josh decided that the two could provide great insight as to why seemingly sane, intelligent human beings could fall for alien stories.

He decided to let the fire die naturally, since there was little danger from it. It was already struggling for its life, and the ground around him was basically dirt. He undressed before climbing into his tent and cozying up into his warm, makeshift bed.

THE MORNING SUNLIGHT in his eyes reminded him why he liked his bedroom so much. Back home, dark curtains and blinds made it easy for him to sleep as late as he desired on a day off. He also missed the blessing of effective pest control. Whatever had been biting him in the night would be addressed with some bug spray, as soon as Josh could find it in the mess of camping gear he'd emptied in his small living space. He rubbed the sleep from his eyes and groped around under his sleeping bag for his phone. It felt like he'd only been asleep for a few hours. He felt the familiar rectangular shape of the device beneath his pillow and pushed the button to check the time.

Two o'clock. How did that make sense? It took a moment for the fact to register in Josh's brain that the bright light outside was caused by something other than the sunrise. Had the old rancher lit up the place with one of his tractors? Or maybe his fire had revived itself? He pondered that idea for a brief moment before he flung his covers back to investigate. He looked through his screen door flap to confirm that the fire was, indeed completely out, yet he could see that a bright glow shone from overhead. Confused, another possibility hit him. Surely, this was not the start of his UFO experience?

"Jesus Christ," he whispered to himself as he reached for the tent zipper. After two hours of sleep, he was hardly in the mood for immature antics. But, he was here to investigate, so investigate he would. He contemplated putting on a shirt or jeans, but then decided that anybody getting him up at two a.m. deserved to see him in his birthday suit. He exited legs first, and scooted his backside out before exposing his head to the bright light. As he scooted, he heard the distinct flutter of a flock of birds taking flight. Josh wondered if he'd just startled a group of free-roaming chickens with his hairy legs. As he brought his head through the opening, the light—lifted. It didn't blink out so much as it rose out of sight into the sky. Odd, he thought. And impressive.

Now there was nothing but blackness, since his eyes were still accustomed to the light. All he could see for the moment was a soft glow from the fire pit, but gradually, other shapes started to appear, ever so slowly, in the foreign darkness. He could see dark shadowy outlines of a few cows nearby, and he noted with a chuckle that they seemed to be perfectly intact. He sat still for another minute until he could see the shape of the barn in the distance. Now he could see the house in the distance, as well as the tree that sat just along the fence line. All seemed well at the ranch, and Josh was just about to climb back into his tent when he heard the fluttering sound again. He looked up to see that it must have been a flock of birds that he'd startled earlier, because the tree was now covered with what appeared to be dozens of peculiar, black images. The shapes were awfully big to be birds. Vultures, maybe? He squinted his eyes and stood up to get a closer look. The one closest to him took form, slowly, but Josh thought his brain must've been playing tricks on him. It looked as if the bird was in a squatting position, with knees jutting up on each side of it. This was no vulture, but Josh wasn't sure what it was. He stepped forward to get a better look, when two eyes came into view. They opened slowly, then blinked. Josh stepped backward, and realized, to his horror, that the other shapes in the tree were taking form. They looked like—gargoyles?

This is a sick trick, he thought. As he tumbled backward, the tree exploded into a cloud of objects that floated in unison out the back of the tree and drifted into the darkness, across the grassy field.

## 13

## FAMILIES AND SUBFAMILIES

"I guess we signed up for crazy town," Josh held his cell phone between his shoulder and chin while he stirred a pot of pinto beans over his campfire. "I mean, we sort of knew, but I'm not sure any of us realized how far some of these people will go to create a hoax."

"Right?" David answered from his end of the line. "For weeks, I've been surrounded by people who are totally convinced that this Sasquatch thing is real."

"So you haven't laid your eyes on one for yourself, yet?"

"Not yet," David laughed. "But my next big adventure is just about to begin. We're heading out West for some secret mission tomorrow, and that will be my big chance, apparently. So tell me about your night. What else happened out on the ranch?"

"Well," Josh said as he settled the wooden spoon on a rock and sat back on his lawn chair. "Not much sleeping happened, that's for sure. After that weird cloud of—things —went floating away, I settled back in my tent and tried to sleep. I did drift off, but I had some crazy ass dreams. Like there were little creatures walking around outside my tent all night. I didn't actually see that, I just heard stuff that made me dream it.

"Probably killer ducks," David said.

"I know, I know. At one point, though, I was half asleep and swore I saw the outline of a creepy hand against the side of the tent. I shot up and it was gone. Man, something was really messing with my head."

"Daaaang," David said. "Sounds you got a fun assignment. You should have some good material for our project. Just figure out how that old guy is messing with your head."

"You think *I* got the plum assignment?" Josh asked in an exasperated tone. "*Me?* You're spending weeks camping in the wilderness with a beautiful TV star, and I'm camping with a chubby truck driver in a cow pasture. How did that even happen?"

David howled. "Dude, you know I'm better looking."

"Screw you," Josh said, which made David laugh even louder.

"But no," David said as he tried to catch his breath. "Seriously," he paused to pant for a few breaths. "I found out this woman actually scammed me before I scammed her!"

"What do you mean?"

"Well," David said. "It seems we weren't the only gate crashers. That first morning at our conference, when I gave my talk, she got nosy and started snooping around. She was apparently intrigued by the title of my presentation. Or maybe I should say she was offended."

"Remind me. Was it 'Story Time?' Something like that?"

"It's only a story. The title was 'It's Only a Story.'"

"Oh, right."

"And, since you apparently were *not* there, I'll remind you that I equated qualitative research to storytelling. Using personal stories, diaries, letters, interviews, testimony: that stuff should not fall under the heading of research material, in my opinion."

Josh had walked right into this mini lecture. David was always willing to give his opinion to anybody who would listen.

"Any conclusions that are not based on statistics," David droned on, "That crap should be called something else, other than research. Calling that sort of material 'research' just further blurs the line between real science and fake news. And fake news destroys civilizations."

"I see," Josh said, partly hoping to cut off his colleague's oration. "So your talk undermines the whole concept of her work. All she has—all any of them have for evidence, is their stories."

"Correct. So when I first approached her, we started off arguing, then things got flirty. She said she'd teach me the importance of personal narrative, so I'm having a good time tagging along. She really is pretty awesome, outside of her crazy beliefs. It's weird. I think I'm really falling for the nut."

"I'm happy for you, man." Josh really was happy for his friend. David was a good guy, but he tended to be rigid. Maybe this chick could lighten him up some. "Listen, buddy. I need to eat my soup beans before they get cold. Have fun on your big adventure and take good notes."

"I'll try," David said. "But, listen, man. I wanted to tell you I've been reading up on your location. You need to be careful. I hear the last team that went to that ranch disappeared without a trace."

"What?" Josh said. "David?" But the other end of the line was silent. Then he realized David was yanking his chain. That bastard had got him again. He stuffed the phone into his back pocket and reached to his cooler to grab a beer before leaning back and closing his eyes. It was funny, the way the guys at the university treated him like a kid brother. He'd never had any brothers; in fact, he never had much of a family at all. He'd been an only child, and he'd lost his parents at a young age. It was nice, the way he was taken in by them. Like they knew he could use a pseudo family.

The warm glow from the campfire flickered and flashed beyond the veil of his eyelids, as he dangled the beer can in one hand. For a moment, he almost forgot where he was. Beyond the crackle from the fire, he could hear an orchestra of crickets singing in unison from somewhere in the distance, and that sound combined with the cool feel of the night air made his mind drift back to the time he had spent many years earlier at summer camp. He remembered being so confident, back then. He had happily conquered all of the scouting challenges with ease, and regularly came in first in the rowing and climbing challenges. Then adulthood happened, and it pretty much sucked. College had been pretty cool, but the part that came after, the decision to take the job at the university, that had been a huge mistake. He had very little time to enjoy himself, and there was the ever present indignation of Crystal that hovered over him constantly. He hadn't really realized how much he hated his life until he'd spent these quiet nights, camping in the tent or spending the night in the cozy barn. He'd had some of the best nights of his life, staring at the sky, talking bullshit with his new friends and drinking beer. This was the life. It was too bad that he seemed to have no answers as to what was going on at this place. He'd pretty much chalked it all up to pranksters messing with the Skylars. Maybe there was something special about the property that made it more valuable than Chet realized, and somebody was trying to run him off.

The *ping* of an incoming message snapped Josh out of

his musings. He mustered up the energy to lift his butt high enough from the chair to retrieve his phone from the back pocket of his jeans, and soon regretted the effort. It was a text from Crystal. A preview bar floated across the top of the screen, and the words "Where the hell are you?" hung there in a hateful green word bubble.

"Kiss my ass," Josh said back to his phone.

"I hope you're not slacking off at some ranch pretending to ..." Mercifully, the preview bubble cut off the rest of the words.

I hate her, Josh thought. It came as a surprise, since he'd never really acknowledged that before, even to himself. Apart from distant cousins, she was just about the only real family he had left, and he wasn't proud of the fact that he despised her. But against the tranquility of the evening in this strange land, her spiteful words made him realize that he truly hated her for the way she belittled him. *If she says one more word, I swear I'm spending the rest of my life as a hermit in the woods*, he thought.

"DO NOT EMBARRASS ME," the next bubble message glowed.

He pressed the off button until the phone screen went dark, and he calmly lifted his rear end from the chair again, and placed the device back into his back pocket.

## 14

## QUESTIONS AND OBSERVATIONS

J osh broke egg number six into the skillet and stirred with a wooden spatula, while Randy Cole described how truck stop prostitution worked. "Not that I ever took advantage," he said," but I'm telling you, some folks made a killin' in the trade.

"Good to know," Josh said. "In case the whole college gig doesn't work out."

"I've always been kind of fascinated about the whole notion of sex being regulated by law," Randy said. "I mean, if aliens really are studying us, they'd be like: 'You paid for *what*? And you went to jail for *that*?'"

"You do have a point," Josh laughed. At that moment, Melanie arrived with a pan full of fried potatoes. "Who is going to jail?"

"Me," Randy said. "For prostitution." He rubbed at his extra large sized beer belly. "It's my retirement plan."

"Good luck with that," Melanie said.

Josh smiled as he continued to stir the scrambled eggs until the mixture was at the perfect, soft consistency. He was a few weeks in, now, and breakfast had become his favorite part of this entire ordeal, since he and the two co-campers had started eating together every morning. Randy and Melanie were both so easy to be around, and they were interesting, as well.

"So anybody got anything interesting to report?" Melanie asked. "I feel like something's about to happen. Just a feeling I get."

"I thought I heard footsteps outside my tent the other night," Randy said, as he scooped a spoon of potatoes into a plate. "I was a little freaked out, so I didn't look."

"Let me get this straight," Melanie said. "You're paying good money to camp out here to see if you can experience anything weird, and you hear a little noise outside and zip yourself tight in your tent?"

"That's about right," Randy laughed. "I'm apparently much braver in theory than I am in practice."

"When was this?" Josh asked. "Because I had a similar experience, on my first night, and I did manage to drag my butt out and take a look. I discovered some big flock of owls or something in a tree."

Melanie gave Josh a sideways glance. "You know owls don't flock, right? I mean, they do gather in small groups called parliaments, but they don't travel at night in big flocks."

"Interesting," Josh said. "I'm really not sure what it was. Maybe condors or something?" He watched as Melanie and Randy looked at each other and raised their eyebrows.

"Joshua," Melanie said in a motherly voice. "I think we talked about this. You are supposed to tell us about anything you experience that could be deemed as unusual. As far as I know, exactly one condor has been spotted in New Mexico in the past fifty years. Would you care to elaborate?"

"I'm sorry," Josh said. He actually did not mind her

playful chiding. He had agreed to be as open as possible about anything he experienced on the ranch, since he'd grown so found of them both. He wanted them to share their insights and experiences with him fully, so he needed to do the same in return. "I'm new at this," he continued. "So, I did wake up in the middle of the night and look out. There was a big flock of unusual looking things filling up that tree over there." He pointed with his spoon. "They looked creepy, but I didn't think they were otherworldly enough to share." He decided to omit the part about the bright light waking him up. He wasn't sure why.

"Josh, I know your stance on this whole paranormal thing, and I respect that," Melanie said. "But I also believe you when you say you'll listen to us with an open mind, when we share our thoughts. So, bear with me for a minute." She chewed for a minute, seemingly looking for the right words. "From everything I've gathered over the years, it seems like Skylar Ranch has a lot more going on than just grey man visitations and cow abductions. This place has long been rumored to serve as some kind of testing ground for—how should I say—experimental creatures."

"What she's trying to say is," Randy interrupted, "there's been reports of some creepy dang critters skulkin' around here at night."

"That is correct," Melanie said. "Animals have been sighted that don't seem native to this planet."

Josh swallowed involuntarily, exposing the awkwardness he was feeling. He liked these two, but he wasn't exactly on the same page with them. He'd have to be careful not to offend them. For the moment, though, he had to admit that the idea of animals from other planets was fascinating. After all, humans had sent everything from mice to monkeys into space for experimentation over the years. Why wouldn't beings from other planets to do the same? "Interesting," he said. "And logical, I suppose."

"So anything weird that happens, we want to know," Melanie said.

"Even dreams?" Josh said. "They've been insane lately." He wasn't sure if it was the atmosphere or his own emotions causing the strange dreams he'd been having, but lately they were lucid and very odd.

"I dreamed about you the other night," Randy said, lifting his eyebrows a few times.

"Please don't tell me any more," Josh said, feigning disgust. "But, seriously, I've had some weird stuff going on in my head."

"Spill it," Melanie said.

"Well, I dreamed I was sitting in this chair, and there were weird little creatures standing around me. They were showing me scenes from my childhood, when I was crying. In one, they were showing me a time when I was real little, and I thought I could get away with stealing the neighbor's new puppy. I was so jealous of that puppy. So anyway, I kidnapped it and put it in my room. Of course, my mom figured it out pretty fast. I had to return the puppy, and it broke my heart."

"No way," Randy said. He looked rattled.

"Seriously," Josh said. "Then they started asking me lots of questions about how I was feeling, like why that whole thing made me cry. It was weird, like they wanted to understand what it was like to be sad. My sadness seemed to frustrate them. It was really creepy, to be honest. Then another time—"

"Don't tell me," Randy interjected. "They showed you a time when your football team moved to Baltimore. It was the Browns, right? They asked you why you were crying and you said you were sad for the whole town."

Josh felt like all the air had left his lungs at once, like someone had just punched him in the chest and knocked the wind out of him. "How the hell did you know that?"

"Because I was there with you," Randy said.

Josh felt sick, like his beer from the previous night was trying to rise back up from his stomach. "Are you two messing with me?" he said. He felt sweat popping up on his face, and his heart was thumping in his chest.

Melanie sat with her mouth hanging open a little and looked back and forth, from Randy to Josh. Her face was pale white. "Gentlemen," she said. "I think you two have had some nighttime visitors."

## 15

## METHODOLOGICAL WEAKNESS

"Dad! Come in here!"

The sound of his son's voice caused Jerry to drop the glass of milk he was holding, allowing it to crash to the kitchen floor, splattering a white flower shape across the slate blue tiles. He ran to Luke's bedroom, where he found the boy curled up in the far corner of his bed. His face was white with fear. "What happened?" Jerry shouted the words, sounding a little more frantic than he'd intended. He wasn't very good at quelling panic, lately.

"It's back," Luke said. He sounded so small, at the moment. "I heard your voice. I thought you said something to me from the bathroom. It sounded like you were calling me in there, so I walked in. You weren't there, so I started to leave. Then there was that really bad smell. And then, when I started to leave, I saw the shower curtain move, like somebody was in the bathtub."

"It's okay," Jerry said. He didn't really know what else to say. He sat on the bed next to his son and wrapped his arms around the child.

"But I saw it, Dad. It pulled the curtain back a little, and there was this blurry image, like it was taking form. It was so scary."

"Listen, son," Jerry said. He was trying to still his own heart to keep from frightening his son even more. "I think you should have gone with Vivian to her mother's house. This was a mistake, you staying here. I'll deal with this thing on my own."

"You can't, Dad," Luke said. "That book said that two or more people have to work together to make him go away. We have to do it together. We just need a bible."

At that second, there was a loud *pop* and the room went dark.

"What happened?" Luke shrieked. Jerry held his son tighter.

"It was just the lamp, son." Jerry was trying to keep his voice from trembling.

"It's not, Dad. It's him." Luke was trying to whisper, but the words came out in a high pitch. "He made the lights go out."

Jerry started to speak, but the words were cut off by a foul smell that seemed to extinguish the breath in his lungs. In the darkest corner of the bedroom, there was movement. To Jerry's horror, a shape began to take form. It was the same, grotesque shape that he'd seen weeks earlier, at the conference. It was about two feet tall, and it had the vague shape of a human, except for the head and neck, which were elongated and lizard-like. The skin was translucent but scaly, and there appeared to be a slime oozing from beneath its scales as the creature rocked back and forth.

Jerry's mind raced. He wanted to run from the room, but he knew his son would not be able to move. He could tell by the rigid feel of his body that he was frozen with fear.

"Do you see it?" Luke whispered.

"Try not to look at it, son," Jerry whispered. "It will go away soon."

As soon as the words were spoken, the thing in the corner started to hiss. It was a low, gurgling hiss at first, then, slowly, the sound increased until it became a growl. The creature took a step forward.

Then it was gone.

Jerry sat holding Luke for several seconds before they both realized that they could move again. The room appeared to be a bit lighter, and the smell was gone. The puddle of slime that had surrounded the creature had also disappeared.

"Dad," Luke said, breaking the silence. Jerry just looked down at his son, hoping he could find words for whatever question might come. "We have to do something," the boy continued. "We need to get rid of it. We have to do the thing."

"I know," Jerry said. "But it will be scary."

"We have to do this," Luke said.

Jerry knew the kid was right.

OF ALL THE things Jerry had planned on doing with his son in his lifetime, an exercise in expelling demons was not one of them. Jerry had decided that they should wait until morning to conduct the ceremony. Even though it would most likely be a while before the creature showed up again, neither of them really wanted to take the chance. He'd also decided that they needed to spend the night in a hotel and get a good night's sleep, because he knew they'd never be able to sleep in that house, after the incident. According to Nilsson's book, all they had to do to get rid of this thing was position some candles around the house and command the entity to leave. Apparently, the little creature would disappear for good, as long as there was a ceremonious command. Jerry should have taken care of this before now, but he kept hoping that everything would stop on its own.

He pulled into the driveway and put the car into park. They sat there in silence, staring at the house. "You don't have to do this with me," he said.

"We're doing this together," Luke said with authority. Jerry couldn't believe how his son was handling this whole thing. He was terrified, himself, and he'd seen a whole damn lot in his life, so he couldn't imagine how his son felt.

"I'll light the candles," Luke said. "We'll do it in the living room, ok? Not my bedroom?"

"Of course," Jerry said. Again, his heart sunk.

Jerry unlocked the front door and entered before Luke, just to make sure nothing was waiting there to jump at them. It was a silly precaution, but it was clear to Jerry that nothing was really out of the question, at this point. As he entered the living room, Jerry could swear there was a heaviness looming in the air. He didn't mention it, but he suspected that Luke sensed it, too, from the concerned look on his face. He took a handful of small candles and placed them around the room, while Luke followed behind with a lighter.

"Dad," he said, as he hesitated at the end of the hallway that led to the bedrooms. "Do you smell something over here?"

Jerry began walking toward the hallway, but the smell hit him halfway there. "I smell it," Jerry said. "Are you ok?"

"Let's hurry and get started," Luke said.

Jerry watched as his son lit the last few candles. He then took Luke by the hand and led him to the middle of the

living room, which glowed softly, now, in the midst of thir-
teen candles.

"The Holy Bible!" Luke said. "We need it!"

Jerry couldn't believe he'd forgotten it. "It's there on the
coffee table," he said. He could swear that the smell grew
stronger with the mention of the Holy Book. He dropped his
son's hand and took three steps toward the Bible. As soon as
his hand touched the Book, a horrific growl exploded in his
ears.

"Dad!" Luke screamed. He was pointing up the hallway.

Jerry followed Luke's gaze, and there on the far end of
the hallway, he saw the creature, looking more putrid than
ever in the full light of day. He could see, now, that it had
long fangs hanging down from its drooling mouth. The
creature took a a step forward, leaving a trail of slime from
its seeping body.

"It's coming!" Luke screamed.

Jerry grabbed the Holy Bible and held it outward,
thrusting it in the creature's direction. In that moment, a
wave of hot air rushed from the hallway, and the front door
burst open. The creature howled and took a few quick steps
forward.

"Run!" Jerry said. To his horror, his son appeared to be
frozen into place. Jerry was shivering all over and weak with
fear, but he knew he had to get his son out of the house. He
managed to rush toward Luke and grab him by the arm. He
pulled the boy behind him as he ran out the front door.
They ran all the way to the car and jumped in.

They sat there panting, side by side.

"You don't have the keys, do you?" Luke asked.

"Nope," Jerry said.

Again, the two sat there in silence, staring in disbelief at their house, until Luke broke the silence. "Are you okay, dad?"

Jerry was caught off guard by the question. He couldn't believe that this was Luke's first concern after the ordeal he'd just been through. He searched for something to say. "Son," he said, his breath still panting. "Did I tell you that I worked at a nudist colony when I was about your age?"

"No," Luke said, with his face twisted in quasi-disgust. Jerry could tell that his son was aghast and confused by his father's inappropriate timing.

"Yeah," he said. "The first week was the hardest."

"You are such an idiot!" Luke said. But Jerry was glowing inside. He'd managed to make his son laugh.

## 16

## CONSULTING THE EXPERT

I t was almost awkward, the way Jerry and Luke sat and stared at each other in silence, communicating only occasionally with eye gestures. The weird little creature had been alone in the house for the past few days, while they'd stayed in a hotel. But today, while they waited for their visitor to join them at the house, they'd both seen it, scampering and darting in and out of the dark corners of the rooms. So they sat there in silence, waiting to see if the *thing* would show itself fully again. It was trying to scare them, Jerry knew, because their fear energized it. He could tell that fear was the creature's nourishment.

"Was that a car door?" Luke asked, breaking the silence and giving Jerry enough of a scare to make him jump.

Jerry twisted his neck around to look out the front window into his driveway. "Nope. It will be a few minutes."

"What's this guy's name, again?" the boy asked. Jerry could hear the nervousness in his son's voice.

"Dr. Nilsson," Jerry said. His mind drifted back to the day, not so long ago, when he'd first heard the man's name, and he'd considered Nilsson to be the biggest crackpot on earth.

Since then, he'd had to face the stark reality that there are things happening in the world that defy explanation and wreak havoc on his belief system.

"You really think he can get rid of this thing?" Coming from his child, the words melted Jerry into a sad little puddle on the couch. He felt horrible for bringing this—whatever it was—into their lives. He had no idea how this experience was going to affect his child in the long run, but he knew the impact would last for the rest of Luke's life, in some capacity.

The most disgusting part was the way it could mimic voices. Visually, it would come and go, but even when it was invisible, it would mimic the voices of their loved ones. Somehow, that intensified the fear. It had been mostly confusing at first, when the voices first started. Jerry would be in his bedroom and hear his wife calling him into the kitchen—but when he got there, he'd realize she wasn't in the house at all. Then it started with Luke. His son would come into the room and ask Jerry why he'd been messing with his head, accusing Jerry of hiding and calling his name. They eventually realized that it was the creature making the voices. And things eventually turned sinister. Jerry was stepping out of the shower one morning when a disembodied voice sounding just like his younger sister made some rather inappropriate comments about his physique. That was the first sign that things were going to get nasty. And then there was Jerry's wife. She'd had a hard enough time trying to believe that Jerry and Luke were seeing some kind of creature lurking around the house, but when she heard the little bastard calling her a dirty bitch using Jerry's voice, things got really interesting. He'd tried to explain everything to her as well as he could, but she was having a pretty hard time wrapping her head around it all. And that was pretty damned understandable, after all. They'd all agreed that it was best for Vivian to go away for a while, so Jerry could work on making this thing go away. The fiasco from days earlier prompted a panicked, humiliating phone call and apology to Dr. Nilsson. Thankfully, Dr. Nilsson responded well. Jerry didn't know what he would do if it weren't for Nilsson.

It was terrifying to know that the man considered this being to be a demon. The methods described in Nilsson's books were actually rituals designed to rid a household of the evil little entities, so Jerry was willing to try anything, but he really didn't like the thought of having a demon in his house. He couldn't believe things had come to this point. He was living a horror film.

The sound of his phone ringing made Jerry jump again. He hadn't felt this nervous since he was a little boy imagining ghosts in his closet. He supposed he'd always had some corner of his mind open to the possibility of paranormal activities, since his mother and grandmother both claimed they could see things others could not. Dead people, to be specific. Jerry had pushed all of that to the back of his mind, long ago.

It was Josh calling. He remembered that Josh was going to get back to him about hallucinations. This was not a conversation that interested Jerry at the moment. Instead of answering, he sent the call to messages.

"Call me when you can, buddy." Josh's words appeared in the message transcript. Jerry had no desire to talk with any of his colleagues at the moment, so he put his phone on silent mode and slipped it into his pocket. It was just a few seconds later that the doorbell announced the arrival of Dr. Nilsson.

Luke must have heard the man pull into the drive,

because he was at the door before the chime stopped ringing. As the man entered the room, Jerry noticed he had the same calm confidence and erudite manner as he'd shown at the conference; the difference was that Jerry was actually willing to show deference to the man this time, and be open to hearing what he had to say. At the moment, he seemed to be the only person in the world who could accept and explain what was happening to Jerry's family.

"I have to thank you for taking the time to come out to meet us," Jerry said, as the man entered his living room. "I'm very grateful—and sorry I didn't listen before."

"Not to worry," Dr. Nilsson said. "I feel responsible. I fear that I inadvertently exposed you to this predicament. These things attach themselves to humans, you see. They can jump around, from person to person. It seems that this particular being found you to be much more interesting than me. May I sit?"

"Of course," Jerry said.

Nilsson rested himself on the couch and placed a large briefcase on the floor beside his foot. "So I understand that you've already made a few attempts to rid yourself of this problem?"

"Yes," Jerry said.

"We did everything you suggested in your book," Luke added. Jerry noted that his kid was handling this subject with courage, so far. A courage that few adults could show in this situation. He was thankful.

"I see," Nilsson said. "But these things are not always so successful, at least not on the first attempts. This is a rite of exorcism, of course. Do you realize that?"

Jerry looked at his son and back to Dr. Nilsson. "I—I realize that this is your theory," Jerry stammered. "I just don't know if I'm ready to label this—thing—whatever it is, just yet. I don't know if I think this is a demon, or if it's some other phenomenon, but I know I want it gone."

"Well, this does help explain why your attempts were unsuccessful," the man said. "You see, I believe that there is a hierarchy when it comes to these entities, just like the hierarchy that exists in the angel realm. Do you see? I think you are dealing with a relatively minor being, when it comes to his gifts and his power, so we may be able to send him home today. However, you *must* carry out your ceremony with a faithful heart. You must be very confident and harbor no fear, and you must believe what you are saying with all of your heart, or the process will not work."

"I'm willing to try your method," Jerry said. "I'll do whatever you ask if it means getting rid of the thing."

"Of course you are willing," Nilsson replied. "This must be very overwhelming for you—both of you." The man gave Luke such a gentle look that Jerry felt a wave of guilt for the disdain he'd felt for the man. "And I'm afraid I'm going to have to ask you about your experiences," the man continued. "I need to understand whom we're dealing with."

"*Whom*?" Jerry asked.

"The name. Every demon has a name, and we must identify the name to gain authority. So I need to ask you to describe what you've seen or experienced."

"He has yellow eyes." Luke blurted, as if he'd been eagerly waiting to impart that information. For some reason, that thought made Jerry nauseous.

"And where have you seen this?" Nilsson asked. He kept his eyes on Luke as he reached into his briefcase. He retrieved a pen and pad, along with a large, tattered book that had most likely been a dark red in its earlier life. Now it was pinkish, with frayed edges. Nilsson set the book beside him on the couch, and Jerry could read the title *Encyclopedia of Demons* written along the edge.

*Of course*, Jerry thought. *How convenient.* Somehow this made his faith falter a bit. He wanted to believe that this man was the real deal, but a catalog of demons was a bit much to swallow.

"I've seen it about four times," Luke started. The quiver in his voice made Jerry realize, once again, that he needed to snap out of his doubts. He had no other choice but to do and believe whatever this man asked.

"The first time, I saw it in my dad's room," Luke said. "Dad was in the hospital and Vivian was spending the night with him."

"Jesus," Jerry said. The thought was unbearable.

"I needed the phone charger," Luke continued. "And it was in their room, so I went in there. I walked over to dad's side of the bed, and I heard a noise from back in the corner, where the window is." He was speaking slowly now, staring at a wall. "It was dark in the room, so I started to turn on the light, but I heard a voice telling me to leave the light off. It sounded like my stepmom, so I stopped. Then I realized the voice was coming from inside the room. I looked over into the corner, and there were those—two eyes."

"And what else did you see?" Nilsson asked as he jotted in his notebook.

"Well, I could only see an outline. The shape looked kind of like a little man, but it was squatting, like those things on top of old buildings. And it had a lizard head."

"Like gargoyles," Jerry added. "That's what I've seen, too. "It seems cliche, I know."

"And other things you've noticed?" Nilsson paused his writing. "I know you mentioned the mimicking. What other abilities does it display?"

"Well," Jerry said. "There is something I should tell you." Jerry realized he was squirming in his seat, feeling like a child who was finally about to divulge a hidden truth to his mother. "I was actually attacked during your session. He either bit me or stabbed me with a weapon of some kind, and my leg has been in pretty bad shape ever since. The doctor said it seemed like a copperhead bite, but with only a small bit of venom?" He felt a little silly mentioning that, but the doctor had held firm that the injury behaved just as a copperhead bite would have. It was still incredibly painful, and it looked like hell, but the nausea and dizziness had subsided.

"Ah," Nilsson said, as he picked up the encyclopedia. "This is very important. Perhaps the entity we're dealing has the ability to interact with nature. As I mentioned, they have different gifts and abilities. It may well have been venom."

"So different demons have different powers?" Jerry asked. He could hear the skepticism in his own voice.

"Yes," the man answered. "Some can change appearances, some can attach to inanimate objects and some to humans, and others can mimic. Some can become solid, while others cannot."

"And some can manipulate objects and consort with snakes?" Jerry said. He was thinking out loud. He was trying to be open.

"That is not my own theory," Nilsson said. "That is the belief of many in the Church, although many others within the faith do not believe in demons, at all."

A sudden *bang* interrupted their talk, as a cup on the coffee table spilled over and sent coffee running across the surface. It had seemed to Jerry that the entire table had lifted and fallen several inches.

"Jesus Christ!" Jerry yelled. At the same moment, Luke

jumped from his own seat and landed beside Jerry. He wrapped his arms through Jerry's.

"What the hell was that?" Luke whispered.

"I believe it was the mention of the Church," Nilsson replied.

## 17

## TWO COSMOI

"This is too scary, Dad. I'm not sure I can do this. I don't want to be here." Luke buried his face in Jerry's arm as he spoke. "I don't think I want to see it again."

"Does he really have to be here?" Jerry wrapped a protective arm around his son and glanced sharply at Dr. Nilsson, as if casting blame on the man.

"Listen," Nilsson spoke directly to Luke. He pulled the boy's hand from the grip on his father's arm and cupped it within his own hands. "This doesn't have to be so frightening. Do me the honor of your full attention for just a moment."

Reluctantly, Luke turned his head toward the man.

"Right now, you are much stronger than this creature is. You mustn't let him make you afraid. That is how he grows stronger."

"But, it's the devil!" Luke said, his voice wavering. "I can't be stronger than him—or it."

"It is *not* the devil," Nilsson said, in a softly chastising voice. "Any more than you are the Creator, himself."

"What do you mean?" Nilsson's words seemed to bolster

Luke's morale slightly. The boy now seemed to relax even more.

"You are a creature of the Realm of Light, and God the Father is your Creator. Do you remember that from my book?"

"Sort of," Luke said. "We mainly just read how to do the ritual."

"I see," the man smiled. "Well, let me remind you of the parts you may have—brushed over." The man leaned closer to Luke and spoke with quiet, but firm, resolve. "There are two realms in creation, you see. One is light and the other is dark. In each realm, there are many entities, some physical and some spiritual, some on this earth and some on other planes."

"Like we have angels?" Luke said.

"Precisely!" Dr. Nilsson said. "That is correct. Like us, angels are beings of the light, but they are some of the most powerful light beings of all." Nilsson glanced at Jerry and flashed a reassuring look before continuing. "It is important to know that beings of Light *always* yield more power, but we, as creatures of Light on earth, temporarily blind to the divine truth, must rely on faith to maintain our power. We must be resolute when we encounter a being of darkness. This creature, here in your home, it has little power. It is a minor being in his world, just as you believe that you are small in your world."

"But he does have powers," Luke said. His words came in a muted challenge. Jerry could tell that the boy wanted desperately to believe the man. "He can disappear."

"*You* have powers. You have much greater powers. You don't consider them powers, because you are so used to them. You have the power to remain in solid form, until your spirit leaves this planet. He envies that."

"He does?" Luke looked up at Jerry, as if to read his face. Jerry smiled and nodded with as much confidence as he could muster. What the hell. It wasn't as if he had a better theory.

"So we can really make him go away if I believe that I'm stronger than him?"

"If you *know* you are stronger," Nilsson corrected. "And we will gain even more power over him when we learn his name."

"Why?" The boy now sounded more intrigued than frightened.

"Imagine you are walking at night in the very dark forest, all alone. You are surrounded by dark shapes, when you hear the most eerie sound you can imagine coming from above. It would be pretty frightening, wouldn't it?"

The boy nodded.

"You might even be frozen in fear. But then, when the clouds part, you see that the sound is coming from an owl. Suddenly, you have lost your fear. You wave your arms, and the owl goes away, more afraid than you were. It is just like *that*. You're no longer afraid, because you have identified the one who has frightened you so. And you realized that you were stronger than he."

As the last word was spoken, the table, once again, lifted a few inches and dropped. Jerry noticed that Nilsson still held tight onto Luke's hand, and Luke only jumped slightly.

"It wasn't so scary that time," Luke said.

"He's nervous," Nilsson said. "He is listening to us, and he knows you're growing braver. Now *he* is afraid."

"Will that book tell us his name?" Luke asked, pointing to the ancient encyclopedia next to Dr. Nilsson.

"I believe it will," Nilsson said. "I think we may have enough clues to determine precisely whom we are dealing with. In fact, I think you should give it a try. If you look into the index under *snake* and *venom*, I think you will be able to narrow down the suspects."

"Cool," Luke said.

"I'll gather the candles," Jerry said.

## 18

## DUPLICATION AND REPLICATION

"I'm sorry, I'm traveling with a moron." Laura's eyebrows made an adorable upside down V shape and her face scrunched ever so sweetly as she spoke to the flight attendant.

"I didn't know what the button was for," David said, fashioning his own eyebrows into the same pose, although he was sure his face was not as cute. He was giddy that the time for their big camping event had arrived. The attendant flashed David a well-practiced, corporate smile and patted him on the shoulder before moving on to check on other passengers.

"I'm sorry!" he whispered to Laura, in a very bad impression of a sorry person. "I've never been in first class before. I'm sure I'll embarrass you a lot before this ride is over."

"People aren't even on the plane yet," she said, feigning disgust.

"I know. This is cool. I was almost the first one on."

"Just ask me before you touch anything else," Laura said. She was so irresistible when she talked down to him.

"You know I'm not that kind of guy," he said. That comment prompted a swat on the arm, which pleased him greatly.

"Here's what we'll do," she said in an annoyed, motherly tone. "We'll go over some rules to keep you busy while everyone finds a seat."

"Go ahead, then. Test me."

"How do we avoid damaging the terrain?"

"No single file walking. Don't step where you step. And stick to rocks and sand when possible."

"Good," Laura said. "No trampling vegetation. And if you get separated from me, what do you do?"

"Blow my whistle. Or flash my little mirror at an airplane."

"And if you're still lost and you need water, how do you find it?"

"Go down hill. Listen for a river. And look for game trails."

"Because trails may lead to a spring," Laura added in a school teacher tone. "Very good."

"What else?" David said, after Laura paused for a minute. "I'm ready."

Laura wasn't answering. She seemed to be staring up the aisle. At first, David thought she was looking at Chaz Galliher, the camera guy, who was half dozing in his seat a few rows ahead of them, but the look on her face was one of concern. She seemed to be staring at the line of people still boarding the plane. "*Damn it,*" she said.

"What's up?" David stood up a little bit in his seat to see whatever it was she saw, but she jerked him back down to his seat. "What the hell?" he said.

"*Shhhh.*" She was now slumping a little in her seat. "I

can't believe this. Those guys were in Winder. At the camp-fire meeting." She was gesturing with her head toward the front of the plane. David managed to take a more discreet look at the people making their way toward them, when he saw a familiar face.

"I know him," David said. "I talked to that guy. That's Kenny."

"I know who the chubby little bastard is," Laura said. She was clearly pissed off. "Did you tell him where we were headed?"

"Of course not," David said. This time the annoyance in their voices was real. "I didn't even know where we were going when I talked to him."

"You're right. I'm sorry," Laura said. "They must have listened in when I was talking to Dr. Wythe, when he was giving me the details. Shit."

At the same moment the words left her lips, Chaz, the cameraman, seemed to recognize Kenny, who seemed to be traveling with two friends. Chaz turned around and mouthed, "What the hell?" to Laura. She shrugged back.

"Hold on," David said. "What makes you guys think that they're headed where we're headed? We're landing in Sacra-mento, but they could be going anywhere. California is a pretty big place."

"Too much of a coincidence," Laura said. "Why would they be traveling the very same day? They want to follow us."

"But why?" As he spoke, the three men were passing by them, grinning sheepishly but avoiding eye contact. Laura kept her eyes locked on them.

"They know I have the best equipment and the best information. They're trying to tag along. They're parasites."

"Is this a thing people do?" David asked. "I mean, don't

they have jobs? How can they afford to take time off work and stalk someone in the wilderness for a chance to catch a glimpse of an elusive ape? I'm not trying to be a smart ass; I'm just trying to understand."

"That's the thing," Laura said. "This is a job for them. Crypto tourism is a real thing. They charge groups a lot of money to take them out camping, with the promise of an exciting experience. These guys are either scouting for a good location, or more likely, they've already arranged to meet a group in Sacramento and are planning to go from there. One of them will trail us and send messages to the group, telling them where to go."

"Good lord," David said. "Just a month ago I was so inno-cent about the world around me." He was only half joking. This was a whole world that had existed while he was happily lecturing in his little bubble of academia. "But I still don't get why it's so tragic. I mean, there's safety in numbers, right? How much harm can they do?"

"David. This is not a game. I am doing serious research, and I'm filming a serious show. They could screw up both. As far as safety goes, they will create more of a hazard, I'm afraid."

"How?"

Laura sighed. "I've told you this before, but I don't think you were listening. Dr. Wythe believes that the recent fires in the Southern regions have displaced several family groups and sent them all on a northerly trek. Sightings have increased all along the state, north of Yosemite. If that's true, they're going to be grumpy, and they're going to be competing for resources. This could be the best opportunity ever for a sighting, but it could also be a volatile situation. If these guys go out there and start beating on trees and leaving food out, they could get us all killed."

"Wow," David said. Laura had insisted many times that there were dangers ahead, but he hadn't taken her all that seriously, except for the normal hazards of wilderness hiking. He'd prepared as much as he could for the possibility of getting lost, or being stalked by a bear or a mountain lion, but he honestly hadn't put much thought to facing a raging clan of displaced ape men, despite her warnings. He was almost concerned. Almost. "I'm sorry this happened," he said. "Maybe you can ditch them?"

"Thanks," she said as she squeezed his hand. "But I doubt it. We're headed for Donner Pass from Sacramento, and there just aren't that many opportunities to shake somebody along that route. I'm pretty sure they'll be able to trail us. We'll just have to deal with them. Damn it."

The sound of an ambulance siren, along with the words Emergency! Emergency! blared from David's phone, causing everyone in his visual range to jerk their heads around and glare, wide-eyed, in his direction. "Oh hell, that's my text tone," he said. He felt the hot blood rushing to his cheeks as he frantically attempted to silence his phone.

"What is *wrong* with you?" Laura said, although he could tell she was trying not to laugh. "We are on an airplane. Did you not think that would be in poor taste at all?"

"I don't get that many texts," David said. "I just forgot. You're the only one who ever writes me." He glanced down at the new message and saw that it was from Crystal.

"Have you seen Josh? He's lost his damn mind," she wrote.

"It's nothing, anyway," David said to Laura, as he shut off his phone. The last thing he wanted to think about was work. He had no intention of getting involved in anything work related, and he was not the least bit interested in talking to his boss at the moment. He wasn't sure why she seemed to obsess about Josh White, and why she hounded him so much, but he just wasn't interested at the moment. The last time he'd talked to Josh, he was sleeping in a tent in the middle of nowhere, gazing at the stars and getting drunk. He was pretty sure that Josh was just fine, right where he was.

## 19

## IMPROVED PROCEDURE

J erry returned to the living room, having strategically placed several holy objects throughout the house, as he'd been instructed by Nilsson. As he meandered through his home, he could hear the man in his living room praying loudly for protection. Luke was joining him. Jerry hoped he had not messed up his kid for life, since he'd raised the kid as an agnostic, but it was not exactly a good time to worry about that. When he entered the room, Dr. Nilsson invited him to sit. "I must tell you what to expect," the man said.

Jerry took a seat beside Luke. "You okay?" he asked.

"I'm good, dad," he said. He squeezed Jerry's hand in a comforting gesture. Jerry had to swallow the lump that developed in his throat.

Nilsson continued. "Please understand that the power to cast away this entity does not come from me; it comes from the authority and Lordship of Christ the King, who has dominion over the dual Cosmoi of Light and Darkness." His tone grew in intensity as he spoke.

Jerry glanced again at Luke, whose eyes were gazing

steadily at Dr. Nilsson. His mouth was hanging open, and Jerry realized that his own was doing the same. The reality of the moment seemed to be hitting them both hard. "Be strong and faithful," Jerry said.

Luke nodded back to Jerry in another attempt to reassure his father.

"You are children of Christ, the Lord of all. You are made in His likeness, from Light, and you exist in the Realm of Light. This entity is from the Realm of Darkness, and there are a few things I want you to know about his presence." Nilsson paused to look them both in the eyes. "First of all, please dismiss from your thoughts all of the dramatic scenes you've seen in movies. You must not fear. Understand that this creature has developed an *obsession* with you both, and with your house. This is not the same thing as a possession. It is a very different thing, indeed. Secondly, you must keep faithful, as I mentioned before. The entity will want to use tricks to break your resolve. However, you must understand that there is a limit to his powers. Do not excite yourself with imagination and conjecture about what he might do. Understand his limitations, and what he *can* do to attack you. Then remove his ability to do that. He can move things, as you've seen. You may expect to see poltergeist-like activity. But know that his ability to manipulate physical matter is very limited, and it uses a great deal of his energy. That energy will not last long."

Jerry had to admit that he was fascinated by the words. "What about another attack of snake venom? Couldn't he kill us with that? And why hasn't he tried that again?"

"Do not imagine that he has abilities that he does not. He cannot conjure snakes, any more than you or I can. He merely has the ability to live among, and be accepted by, venomous snakes." He smiled and looked at Luke. "Do you have any venomous snakes on your property?

"Not that I'm aware of," Jerry said.

"When you were in Savannah, the entity most likely did have access to, and was able to dwell among, a variety of swamp-dwelling snakes. He simply has not had the opportunity to replenish his toxic weaponry in this location."

"Fascinating," Jerry said.

"There is one more thing to keep in mind." Nilsson paused and looked back and forth at Jerry and Luke, as if to emphasize the seriousness of his next words. "He may reveal your secrets, in an effort to shake you."

"Like, what secrets?" Luke said nervously, before Jerry could ask the same.

"Embarrassing or damaging secrets may be revealed. These entities have been known to reveal things that may cause you distress. This is a tactic that often works to break the flow of faith. I tell you this now, because we must keep the flow of faith strong."

"I want to say something," Luke said with a nervous eagerness. Jerry wanted to stop his son, but the boy continued before Jerry could intervene. "I've looked at naked girls. On the internet."

Dr. Nilsson smiled kindly, and Jerry's eyes flooded with tears. He felt joy and pride and sweet regret at the same time. He was proud and somewhat sad that his son had just been brave enough to reveal his darkest secret, but it was mixed with the relief that this actually *was* his darkest secret. It must have seemed so monumental, in front of this man of faith. "I love you, kid," Jerry said.

"And I'm very proud of you for that." Nilsson said sweetly to Luke, but his expression changed abruptly. Jerry knew from the man's sudden change that he must have realized how odd his words sounded—or would have sounded under ordinary circumstances. "For the confession, not the deed," Nilsson clarified. The laughter, fueled by the tension in the air, erupted spontaneously, as they all realized the absurdity of the situation.

"It would be weird if you were proud of me for looking at girls." the boy laughed.

"These are strange times, indeed," Nilsson joked. He paused and looked at Jerry with his serious tenor returning. "And you? Do you have concerns that this entity will attempt to break your faith with a revelation? Do we need to talk in private before we proceed?"

Jerry thought for a moment. "I cheated on my taxes," he said, barely keeping the grin from his face. Again, the room erupted with laughter.

"I have to say," the man said with the gentlest voice Jerry had ever heard, "You two are certainly making this process easier than normal."

"We're pretty boring," Jerry said. Again, Nilsson returned to his stern manner.

"Have you asked others to pray for you at this time?"

"My mother is," Jerry said. He felt his face flush as the words left his mouth. It had been an odd conversation, the previous day, when Jerry had called his mother and asked if she could do him the favor of praying for his protection. The woman had been suspicious and gleeful at the same time, since she'd tried to lure him into church for all of his adult life. She'd tried her best to get Jerry to explain his request, but he'd managed to put her off. "I'm sure she's been praying nonstop."

"And Vivian," Luke added. "I asked her to pray." This time, Jerry squeezed his son's hand. For as long as Jerry had known Vivian, she'd been a resolute agnostic.

"Excellent," Nilsson said. "Now we must begin. And for review, I'll first isolate the creature in this location so he can't escape, and then I'll banish him to the dark realm."

Jerry listened as the man began to chant a series of prayers. He tried to concentrate on the man's words, but he kept getting distracted by sounds coming from other rooms. It was probably his imagination, but he thought he heard knocks coming from his bedroom. He looked at Luke, and realized he was also glancing down the hallway. Jerry tried hard to stay calm and pay attention to Nilsson's prayers.

A loud *bang* from the kitchen made him jump, along with Luke. It was the sound of a cabinet door swinging open.

"Remain calm and faithful," Nilsson said. "And strong." He continued with his words, notifying the entity that, under the authority of the Almighty, he was now summoned to the interior of the living room, where he would be confined.

At this point, Jerry heard a low hissing sound coming from behind the television. It grew louder in intensity. Luke looked at Jerry, wide eyed, and Jerry tried to muster a calm face while he winked at his son.

"You are powerless," Nilsson said in the direction of the hissing sound. "You must obey the commands which are expressed with the authority of Jesus Christ, the son of God."

The hissing sound increased and then transitioned to a raspy, growling noise, breathing in and out like a rabid dog. Jerry felt himself trembling, and stared intensely at Nilsson to block out all noise except for the man's words.

To Jerry's right, the television took a violent jerk forward and fell from its base, and the crashing noise coincided with a loud growl. The sound startled Jerry, but he realized in an instant that the sound was not so terrifying as the vision that was now appearing beside the wreckage on the floor.

It was a vibrating haze, taking the shape of the sickening, troll-like creature. He tried to concentrate as Nilsson challenged the creature to walk forward. It began moving forward, and as it approached them all, its form became increasingly solid. Jerry felt numb in every part of his body. He tried to swallow, but he couldn't command his throat to work, and his mouth remained open as the creature moved closer and closer. He realized, as its eyes became more defined, that it was looking straight into his own. Step by step, it came toward him, looking straight into his eyes, with yellow pupils with slits that resembled a snake's. The growl was loud and gurgling.

"Remain calm and faithful!" Nilsson shouted. "He has no power over us!"

Jerry wanted to look at his son, to try to comfort him and keep him from being terrified, but he could not control his gaze. He could not tear his eyes away from the gaze of this entity, and he began to feel helpless. As it stepped closer, the vibration slowed and the creature became more and more solid in horrible appearance. It was only three feet from Jerry now, and it stepped forward again and stopped. As Jerry watched, it drew a deep, raspy breath. It began to speak.

"*Your frieeends,*" it said in a slow, evil, growl. "*They think they are so cleverrrr... They are going to die...*"

Jerry began to shake uncontrollably. In his peripheral vision, he saw Nilsson extending his arms, reaching toward the creature with open palms. "I know your name!" he shouted. "You are Naga, and I command you to return to the Realm of Darkness, to wait there until your judgement comes." The creature kept his gaze on Jerry, but he was starting to vibrate again. Nilsson was now screaming his words. "In the name of Jesus Christ, the King of All, the son of the Creator, you must return now!"

The creature vanished.

Jerry stared at an empty patch of carpet and tried to close his gaping mouth, which, he realized, was sticky and dry. Slowly, he managed to regain control of his movements, but it seemed like he could only manage one function at a time. He closed his mouth, managed to swallow, and turned his head to look at Luke. His son was also staring, eyes wide, at the patch on the carpet.

"It's over," Nilsson said. "Do you feel the lightness in the air?"

It was true. Jerry hadn't noticed until now, but there had been a heaviness in the air that seemed to have lifted. "Are you okay?" he said to Luke.

"*Dad!*" was all he could say in response, at first. After a few seconds, he continued. "Did you see that thing?"

"I did, son. Are you okay?"

"I think so. Dad, that was weird."

"I'm so sorry, son," Jerry said as he nearly leapt from his seat to embrace Luke. He felt sick from having created this bizarre situation, and he felt the tears stream down his face.

"I'm okay, dad. It's okay." The boy was hugging Jerry and patting him on the back.

"You will both be fine, now," Nilsson said. "He is banished, and he cannot return."

They all sat in silence for several seconds before Jerry spoke again. "Can I ask you some questions?" he said to Nilsson.

"Of course you may."

"That creature," Jerry said. "That was a demon. Are they all demons?"

"What do you mean by *them all*?" Nilsson asked, as he slowly closed a small prayer book and set it on the couch beside him.

Jerry searched for words, but he didn't know what to say. The thing *knew*. It knew that Josh and David were somewhere out there putting themselves in danger. "It said my friends are going to die," Jerry said.

"I assume he was playing on your fears," Nilsson said.

"I don't know," Jerry said. "I think it knew something. I think it knew what my friends are up to."

"What are your friends up to?" Nilsson asked.

Jerry realized that he needed to have this conversation with Nilsson outside of Luke's ear shot. His kid had learned quite enough, for now.

"Can I walk you to your car?" Jerry asked.

## 20

## BAD EXPERIMENTS

"Oh, dear," Nilsson said, as he deposited his brown leather case into the back seat of his car. "You are saying that your friends have intentionally set off to encounter these creatures?"

"I'm afraid so," Jerry said. "I'm afraid we've all done something really stupid. I'm actually terrified, because that —*thing*—I think it knew. It said my friends are going to die, and now I'm feeling sick, because it seems that my friends are out there chasing demons. Is that true? I mean, have I got the gist of the situation here?" Jerry could hear the sarcasm, as well as the desperation, in his own voice.

"Somewhat true," Nilsson said, as he leaned back on the side of his car and crossed his arms. "It would be impossible for me to explain my entire hypothesis to you in the next few minutes. I can only try to tell you what I believe I have uncovered, in a very basic way. Some of it, I'm very certain about. The rest—we cannot know for sure."

"I'd appreciate it," Jerry said. "I'm scared shitless here. For my friends. Pardon my language."

"Well," Nilsson said, and then rubbed at his chin as if he

were trying to determine how to begin. "As I've mentioned to you before, I am of the opinion that two contrasting cosmoi, or realms, exist, and the beings of these realms have been in battle since the beginning of creation—that is, creation as human beings understand it." He looked at Jerry as if to gauge whether to continue. Jerry must have passed the test, since Nilsson did carry on, after a few seconds of hesitation. "We see evidence of these warring cosmoi from the lore and the early writings of all of the world's religions, in all the far corners. And, by the way, you may call these cosmoi anything you like. Some people may refer to these as dimensions, for example. For clarification purposes, I often refer to them as realms of dark and light."

"I remember that from earlier," Jerry said. "So God is from the light cosmos and the devil rules the dark one?"

Nilsson smiled. "Religion is a social construction; it fits within our limited perception, so we will go with that for now. In fact, this is why I equate cryptid creatures to demons. It's the simplest way for humans to understand this phenomenon."

"But you're a priest," Jerry said. He was a little baffled that Nilsson seemed to be scoffing a bit at the notion of organized religion, especially after the events of the day, but he was in no position to question the man's abilities at the moment.

"True," Nilsson said. "But my beliefs stretch a bit further than the Church would prefer."

"I see," Jerry said.

"Now—it is important to know that each realm has entities that dwell in spiritual form, and some that exist in physical form. And some can exist, to some extent, in both forms, like the entity you had in your house."

"I think I follow," Jerry said. "Like we have angels and

ghosts and mortals on the good side." He wasn't sure he was buying it all, but he was trying to lead Nilsson to his point more quickly.

"And, so," Nilsson said, seeming to pick up on Jerry's angst. "Warriors from these realms have raged their battles in spirit form for millennia, because spirit is the natural and most common state of beings, both light and dark. We're all spirits, and the physical world we live in at the moment is only a temporary, unsustainable pause in the journey of some souls in the Realm of Light. We come here, to this physical life, to feel our way through the darkness and to grow, in a spiritual sense. We grow through faith."

Now Jerry was really growing impatient. "So what does this mean? Are my friends out there chasing real monsters from hell?" he asked. He needed to know if Josh and David were in immediate danger, and he also needed to get back to Luke, who was now sitting all alone inside the house after a spectacularly traumatic experience.

"I believe that the ruling entities from the Realm of Darkness are growing weary of the spiritual battle. I believe they have discovered that it might be more effective to bring their battle to the physical world," Nilsson said. "The earth is like an incubator, and they desire to crush the eggs, you could say. In other words, if you want me to be direct, I think they are creating monsters and placing them in this physical plane, to do their bidding."

"Creating monsters." Jerry had to repeat the words to help them sink in.

"To be precise," Nilsson continued, "I believe that the aliens you mentioned—I believe your friend Josh is seeking aliens—they are actually the ones creating physical monsters, through physical experimentation. I believe that they—being physical entities from the Realm of Darkness—

have been meddling with earthly DNA for thousands of years. Evidence of this also exists in ancient texts. The Bible, for example, states that the fallen angels came to earth to mate with human women and the result was the Nephilim. Some actually believe that the Sasquatch and the Nephilim are one and the same. Every civilization has stories of beings from the sky, coming to earth and whisking away or otherwise having their way with humans. Did you know that many of the European fairies were first described as grey creatures with large, almond shaped eyes?"

"And they're creating monsters and leaving them here on earth?" Jerry was still trying to cut through the weeds and get some kind of understanding. At the same time, he knew there was no way in hell that he would be able to convince Josh and David of any of this. "Why would they have to do that? If they're so advanced, why can't they just zap us, like in the movies?"

"Again, this is not Hollywood. I believe that the creatures we call aliens cannot survive in the earth's atmosphere. They probably don't *zap* us because they don't want to destroy the planet, they just want to destroy the inhabitants. And they have never been able to do much about it, except to lead humans astray through fear and spiritual influences. But, after centuries of experimentation, now they are creating hybrid creatures that actually could wage a physical war. If you do a quick internet search, you'll see that cryptid sightings are becoming quite common. In fact, they're growing at an alarming pace."

"So all these claims of monster sightings, Sasquatch, the Mothman, the Dogman—those have been alien experiments?"

"What we know as cryptid creatures are either of two things: they are either naturally evolved animals that come from the planets in the dark realm—I believe the black dog and the black panther sightings in the US are examples of those—or they are experimental beings, designed for wicked purposes. The latter are created with a mix of materials, or DNA, from different worlds. These aliens have long sought to create an army of beings that will fight a physical battle to match the spiritual battle, and I believe that the Sasquatch has been their most successful creation. In fact, they may be the Nephilim reinvented. It is said that the originals were killed in the great flood. At any rate, the ultimate point, I believe, is this: The Realm of Light has always been the most powerful realm. This recent invasion of cryptids is an attempt to destroy the place where spirits of light come to grow. It is rather ingenious."

Jerry didn't know what to say for several seconds, but he wasn't quite finished questioning Nilsson, yet. The implications were terrifying, if any of this was true, but he had no reason to doubt the man at this point. "Nilsson," he said. "Do you think my friends are in serious danger?"

"Oh, I am fairly certain they are," Nilsson said, as he swatted at an insect circling his head."But those sorts of beings are out of my wheelhouse. I think you must do what you can to bring your friends home, very soon."

## 21

## ANECDOTAL EVIDENCE

L ife was excellent.

David stretched out his arms and breathed in the morning smells of damp pine bark and campfire smoke. He turned to his side as he stretched, to see a lumpy pile of forest green polyester about two feet away. Inside that lump was the loveliest creature he'd ever known.

He had to admit he was smitten. Laura was so passionate about her work, and so endearing when she was passionate. He could understand why her TV show was such a hit. He'd learned, over the past several weeks, to compartmentalize his feelings about her field of work and his romantic feelings. He'd been having the time of his life, tagging along on the mysterious trek through the wilderness while Laura and her cameraman searched for signs of a great beast. So far, there had been no sign of footprints and no opportunity to use the little plaster casting kit, which disappointed him a little. He'd been awarded the job of making footprint casts, but so far, the journey had yielded no such evidence. But not all was lost, as far as Laura was concerned, because they had stumbled upon a few teepee-like structures made of big sticks. Laura and her coworker had been excited to find those, but to David, they looked a lot like the stick houses he and his neighbor kid had made twenty years earlier, as preteens playing under the trees of his Ohio back yard.

Despite the disappointing lack of monster sightings, the summer was shaping up just as he had hoped. He'd been able to play wilderness man while Laura and Chaz stopped every few hours to observe and record any suspicious looking tree branches. They were making pretty slow progress through the woods, be he didn't care. He could tell that Laura was growing increasingly anxious about the lack of any exciting findings, though.

David wasn't at all sure where they were, exactly, although he knew they were somewhere north of Donner Lake. They'd stayed at the lake in a cabin for a few days while Laura and Chaz collected supplies and coordinated with producers and Dr. Whythe. All David knew was that they were going north, and that their plans were sort of sketchy and secret, because they were going off trail, whatever that meant. He assumed they were crossing though some private lands or government property that was otherwise off limits. Conversations were pretty hush, hush, so David kept mum about it all. He just went along for the experience, and assumed that if they got into any legal trouble, the network would provide some heavy legal support. Mainly he kept his mouth shut and helped with chores.

He stretched again and realized that he really needed to get up for a whiz, but the thought of getting up was annoying. It was way too cozy in the downy comfort of his sleeping bag, and the mountain air was hovering somewhere in the forties, a temperature that was perfect for snuggling with a beautiful woman, but not so great for a walk in the nude. David rubbed at his itchy eyes, propped himself on one elbow, and stared down at the woman sleeping next to him. She was also naked, he knew. She'd managed to sneak away into her own sleeping bag sometime after he fell asleep— her little way of remaining independent, he figured. He reached over and peeled back the cover to reveal her face.

She looked so beautiful, laying there with her head twisted toward him, breathing heavily as her long hair splayed across her pillow. *Damn it,* he thought. How the hell did he get himself into this? The physical stuff was mind blowing, for sure. But the big problem was that he genuinely liked her company. He'd never laughed so much or had so many interesting conversations as he did with her. He really dreaded the day when he'd have to ruin it all, when they finally hit that wall. She'd never forgive him when he turned this adventure into a conference talk, when he would expose the truth about this excursion and disparage her livelihood. But it was unavoidable. Even if his heart wasn't in it, his friends would expect him to hold up his end of the deal. He couldn't see any way out of it. *What a bastard you are*, he thought to himself.

Laura stirred and brushed the hair from her face, seeming to sense his stare. She mumbled something before turning her back to him, revealing the bare curve of her spine. He wanted to reach out to her, but he was reminded from his full bladder that he was in no shape to start any such thing at the moment.

He unzipped his own sleeping bag and threw back the flap, exposing his entire, naked body to the chilly air. His shoes had somehow managed to travel a few feet beyond his reach in the night, so he stepped naked into the cold air to fetch them and rushed back to the warmth of his bag. Without being cheesy, he had to admit that the night before had been exquisite. Luckily, Chaz preferred to sleep in his tent, set far away from theirs, and he preferred the cold night air, so he always pitched it a good distance away from the fire. So the previous night, the sky had been amazingly clear, and the stars were so brilliant that they had decided to lay outside in the open, alone by the fire, chatting and exploring one another for hours. Laying there, exhausted, snuggling with this beautiful woman, seeing a mountain view of the cosmos for the first time, smelling of smoke—he had experienced perfection.

He finished tying his shoe and headed for the nearest tree, but then had second thoughts. He didn't want *that* to be her first sight when she opened her eyes: his bare-naked butt shining in the early morning light. Besides, he needed to pass gas, and it was sure to come bursting out with a trombone sound as soon as he applied any pressure, and that she certainly didn't deserve. He was already exposed to the cold air now, so he made his way through the dense brush and trees to find a giant tree to step behind. There was a big one, about twenty feet into the thicket, with a trunk wide enough to hide his entire body, so he happily skirted around the tree trunk and directed old one-eye toward the base and enjoyed the bliss of emptying his bladder.

A pee tingle shuddered through his body, which was exhilarating for a second, but the momentary joy was interrupted by *whack* sound and a simultaneous sharp pain on his right shoulder blade. It felt like he'd been stabbed, right behind his arm socket, and as it happened, he'd seen a fist-sized rock ricocheting off his body and tumbling to the leaves. "What the fuck?" he yelled as he grabbed at his shoulder. He wheeled around toward the forest behind him, but saw only a few slight waves of leaves in the breeze. "Who's out there?" he yelled as he felt around for blood. "Are you fucking kidding me?" He yelled toward the woods, not caring that the person he was yelling at was most likely the lovely lady he'd just left in a sleeping bag. This was apparently her idea of some joke, throwing a rock at him while he was distracted by a penis in his hand. What the hell was she thinking? He finished relieving himself and stomped back toward the camp site, holding his sore shoulder with his left hand. He wasn't amused with her attempted play, even though he was pretty sure she hadn't really intended to hit him. He tried to calm the anger that pulsated through his veins, but it wasn't easy. It was a foolish move on her part, and he had every right to be pissed. So much for the perfect lover he'd found. He made his way back to his sleeping bag and kicked off a shoe in a violent flick of his foot, letting it fly through the air, not caring where it landed. It landed square on the lumpy bag containing Laura's body.

"Ouch," a muffled voice sounded from within the fabric. Laura's face emerged from the open end. "What the hell was that?" she said.

She looked genuinely confused, and barely awake.

"You're shitting me, right?" David said. He was still angry, but also a bit confused. Either she was a really good actor and a really fast runner, or somebody else had just pelted him with that rock.

Laura sat up half way and looked around for several seconds in what appeared to be a genuine daze. "What's going on?" she asked. "Did-did you just throw your shoe at me? What the hell?"

"Seriously," David said. "Are you messing with me? Because somebody just threw a rock at me, and I thought it was you. Was it?"

David could tell that it was taking Laura some time to process this information. "So somebody threw a rock at you and a shoe at me?" she said. She was genuinely confused and half awake. Plus, her boobs looked exquisite as she reclined there, propped up by her elbows and exposed from the waist up.

"Forget the shoe," he said. "That was me, but it was an accident. But look at this." He twisted his torso around so she could see his shoulder blade. "Is there a mark?"

"Jesus," she said. "There's a welt. What happened?"

"It was a rock!" he yelled. "I was taking a whiz on a tree over there and somebody threw a rock at me." As soon as the words left his mouth, he realized what was going on, and the anger started to return. "Hang on," he continued. "Was it Chaz?" With that, he marched as sternly as he could, considering he was now naked and wearing a single shoe, and unzipped Chaz's tent flap without warning the guy. He was pretty sure he'd find the tent empty, since the guy would have had no opportunity to climb back in, unseen. But as he poked his head inside the tent, his eyes adjusted to see a sleepy-eyed Chaz looking up at him in confusion.

"What the fuck, dude?" he said. He looked up at David in all his nudity, with a look of horror and shock.

"Sorry," David said, and backed out slowly, zipping the flap back into place. He could hear a muffled "What's the matter with you" as he backed away from the tent. There was just no way that Chaz had been the culprit. He turned back to Laura—and then another thought occurred to him. "It's those assholes from the plane," he said.

"I have no idea what you're talking about, David. You're being irrational."

"I'm talking about this," he turned to display the red mark on his shoulder. "Somebody threw that rock. They don't fall from trees."

"Oh my god," she said, gazing back toward the woods

and looking more fully awake. As soon as the word left her mouth, another object landed between them with a *thud*. It was a another rock, this one was bigger than David's head, and it seemed to have fallen down from the sky. "Oh this is absurd," he said, jumping to his knees. "This shit is not funny." He climbed over Laura and grabbed at his discarded shoe as she emitted some squealing grunt of disapproval. She could act offended all she wanted, for all he cared. He was pretty sure that some of her Sasquatch compatriots were skulking around out there in the woods trying to scare him. He got to his feet, still holding the second shoe in his hand. "Who's out there?" he yelled. As he stood there, another huge rock came tumbling from the tops of the trees, missing him by a few feet and landing with a thud. "Sons of bitches!" he yelled again toward the tree line, this time stomping in the general direction of the rock's trajectory. He'd only made it a few feet when a his ankle twisted with a jolt. "*Damn* it!" he screamed. He hobbled back toward the campsite, fighting the urge to cry. His ankle wasn't too injured, but his pride was. Laura was there, hovering over the large rock that had landed between them, snapping pictures from her camera.

"What are you doing?" he asked. He heard the venom in his own tone, but he didn't care. "Are you freakin' kidding me?" She was on her knees, still nude, wedging a stick under the rock to observe beneath it, treating it like she'd just unearthed some golden trinket from the Amazon.

"David, I need you to calm down." Her voice sounded urgent. She bent low and snapped a few more photos of the rock's underbelly. "This is serious."

"I'm seriously going to kick somebody's ass."

"Shut up and *listen*," she said as she placed her camera on the ground and turned to him with more anger in her face than he'd ever seen. "Something is happening here, and I need you to calm down and work with me. And think rationally for a second."

"Rationally?" He was still dripping the sarcasm. "Meaning what?"

She was feeling around the depths of her sleeping bag and pulling out yesterday's clothing. "Well..., why don't you come and try to pick up this rock..., for one thing." She was now trying to stand up while thrusting her legs inside her jeans as she spoke in sharp, angry bursts. "And see how far you can toss it in the air." She yanked the jeans over her hips and fastened them as she stared. "Well?"

He glanced down at the mini-boulder and grasped her meaning in an instant. The rock would have been way too heavy for him to toss more than a few feet, and even that might put his back out. He headed toward it anyway, just to see how it felt to lift it up. As expected, it felt like heavy gym weights. Somehow, this had fallen from the treetops.

"It's some trick," he said, but his mind was grasping for a reasonable explanation. "They've got a catapult or something." It sounded absurd as he said it. They were miles from civilization, including any kind of road, and in the rough terrain, the woods were way too dense to maneuver any type of machinery.

"Really?" Now she was sounding sarcastic.

"I don't know how they did it, but this is some stupid trick. They're trying to scare me, because I'm a professor and I'd add credibility to the whole Bigfoot claim."

"What?" she seethed. There was a purple vein trying to burst from her forehead. "Are you really serious?" Now she was yelling.

"I'm not saying you are in on it..." he stammered.

She didn't let him finish. "Do you have any idea what

kind of people are involved in this type of study?" She was now jerking a shirt over her head in a furious tantrum. "You think you're special because you work at some state university?" That was a low blow. "You really are something. I don't have time for this."

"Okay, let's both calm down," he said. He realized it was time for him to put on his own clothes, because he felt ridiculous enough having this argument, without suffering the added vulnerability of nakedness. He fumbled around inside his sleeping bag to retrieve his own pants and had one leg inside when he felt his sore shoulder hitting the ground, right before his head hit the dirt with a *thwack*.

He had fallen. There was a sharp pain in his head, and the world was vibrating around him.

In a haze, he realized he was lying on his left side in the dirt with his intestines shaking violently inside him. His entire body pulsated, and everything around him went dark. His brain scrambled to make sense of what was happening, but nothing made sense. He was paralyzed and vibrating at the same time, unable to gain control of his body and unable to see anything outside a small circle of awareness. His throat ached like it was screaming, but he couldn't hear whether it was or not. He maneuvered his eyes toward Laura, who was on her knees and crouching to hold her head beneath her arms. He had no idea what was happening. Nothing made sense. Was it an earthquake? He couldn't focus, and then everything was still and silent. He lay there for a second, frozen in confusion, and saw that Laura, too, was unable to move from her position.

It wasn't until he heard the quiet that he realized that the cause for the past several seconds of chaos had been a deafening sound that was so loud that it reverberated through the ground and his entire body like a seismic event.

"Get in the tent," Laura yelled, as she scrambled on hands and knees. Her voice was muffled so that she sounded a mile away. The loud noise had deafened him.

"WHAT THE HELL WAS THAT?" David could hear the quiver in his own voice as he huddled with Laura inside the small tent.

Laura didn't answer. She was sitting with her arms wrapped around her knees, rocking back and forth with her green eyes bulging to double their normal size. She was trembling so hard that David thought she might topple over at any moment. "Are you okay?" he asked. No matter who or what was responsible, this shit was scary enough, without her wigging out on him.

"I'm fucking excellent," she answered. "I told you about the rock throwing and the...sound thing. It was in the book. This is incredible!"

"Listen," he said. He was a little wigged out by her crazed behavior. "I don't want to argue or anything, but whatever made that sound was batshit nuts. I mean, I thought I'd been hit by some atomic wave. What the hell was it, for real?"

"They're warning us," she said. Her voice was coming in short breaths. "They're really here! If we stay in here and don't antagonize them any more, we should be okay." She seemed to believe what she was saying.

"You want to *stay* here? Are you serious?"

"Of course I'm serious," she said, turning to look into his eyes with a maniacal stare. "This is what I came here for." Her voice had the shrill tone of tight vocal chords. "I think if we just show deference to them, we will be fine. I just need to get a grip for a minute." She gave an embarrassed chuckle. "I mean, I have heard all about their roar, or scream, or whatever you call it, but still. Obviously, I wasn't totally prepared for that."

"Well I sure wasn't prepared for that, either. But listen. Don't get mad at me. I just can't wrap my head around the whole Sasquatch thing. I know you believe it with all your heart, darling, but I think somebody is really messing with us. Where's the gun?"

"In the bag, there," she pointed. "But listen. Don't shoot unless they come close and act aggressive. I don't think they want to hurt us."

"Come into the camp? I'm shooting like a freakin' wild man if I get hit by another one of those boulders," he said.

Laura grabbed his wrist and squeezed so hard he felt the blood struggling to pump through her grip. "Listen to me," she said. "Don't do anything to antagonize them. I think this started because you peed on a tree. They thought you were marking your territory. Just please do what I say from now on. Don't wander off too far to relieve yourself. Keep it within our clearing, pretty much."

"Well, that's pretty gross," he said. "I'm not pooping in our camp, just so you know."

"And don't make any loud banging noises trying to scare them away. And keep the fire small. They might be nervous about the fire. Let's just lay low for the next few hours. I'm pretty sure they don't want to hurt us, or they would have by now."

"Well, I'm not so sure about 'them' not wanting to hurt us," he air quoted the *them*. Those weren't bouquets they were tossing our way." As he spoke, he reached across Laura to retrieve the bag containing the gun.

"But they didn't hit us, at least not with the big ones," she said. "They could have, I'm pretty sure."

"Then what?" he asked as he examined the handgun he was now holding. "We sit here a few hours and then what happens?" He wasn't sure what she was trying to accomplish.

"Then we wait and see if they start to show themselves. If we're lucky, they'll get curious and start coming close."

## 22

## PHYSICAL EVIDENCE

"We should check on Chaz," Laura said. "It's weird that we haven't heard from him." She spoke in an urgency that made it clear that she'd forgotten about the man's existence. Once they'd gathered enough wits to get properly dressed, the two of them had been sitting in silence for the past fifteen minutes, listening for footsteps or other signs of life. David assumed that Laura had been stunned and lost in thought, as he had been.

He had no idea how anyone could have produced the effects they'd just experienced out in this wilderness. Then again, he wasn't a magician, but he knew they could pull off some impressive illusions. Whatever was actually going on, he'd decided he wasn't going to push the issue with Laura any longer. Maybe she was being duped by her producers. Who knew.

"Want me to check on him?"

"Please?" she asked.

David unzipped the tent flap and stuck his head into the fresh air. The world around him seemed normal enough at first glance, especially in contrast to the strange ordeal he'd just experienced. But something was off. He pushed his way out and perused the campsite again. Something was different, but he wasn't sure what. The large rocks were still there, where they'd landed, and David noted again that there was no way a human could have been responsible for sending them flying through the air. They gave the campsite an eerie feel, like their mere presence represented something deeply sinister, but that wasn't what was bothering him. He couldn't put his finger on the strange feeling in the air.

As he made his way toward Chaz's tent, he realized what was bothering him. It was the *silence*. There were none of the usual sounds of birds or insects; even the wind seemed to have stopped rustling the leaves in the trees. There were no sounds of planes flying overhead and no sounds of squirrels scampering. It was an impossible silence.

David reached Chaz's tent, which was zipped tight. "You okay in there?" he called.

There was no answer.

"Hey, buddy," David said. He poked at the front of the tent. "Laura wants me to check on you. You okay?"

Still nothing.

This is irritating as shit, David thought. He grabbed the zipper and wound it around to create an opening. When he stuck his head inside, however, he saw tree trunks. His brain stretched for an explanation. *Why was he seeing trees inside the tent?* After a half second of confusion, it dawned on him that he was gazing straight through a gaping hole in the back side of the tent. The back wall was completely shredded.

"Chaz!" David screamed as he pushed his way back outside. His head was pounding along with his rapid heart beat. He turned in every direction and yelled into the forest, calling out the name. "*Chaz!* Where the hell are you?"

"Is he gone?" Laura said as she appeared beside David. "He's not in his tent?"

David could hear the panic in her voice. This was not an act. Whatever was happening in these woods, she was not involved. He was certain. He grabbed her and pulled her tight. "Listen, babe." He tried to keep his voice steady as he spoke. "I don't know where he is, but I'll find him."

"Are you sure he's not in here?" She pulled away and bent toward Chaz's tent before David could stop her.

"Don't go in there!" David said. He reached for her, but she was already poking her head inside. She fell backward again. Her hands were over her mouth, and her eyes were bulging open.

"Oh my God," she squealed quietly. "Oh my God."

David sat beside her and pulled her close again. His mind raced and he started babbling in an effort to comfort her. "Listen," he said. "I can explain this. Have you ever heard of that incident in Dyatlov Pass? Those kids?"

"Yes," she whispered in a high pitch. "And they were found dead."

"Yes," he said. "*But* remember how they cut their way out of the side of their tent with a knife?" David was pretty impressed with the theory he was inventing on the spot. His panicked mind seemed to be operating at some new level. "Some people say they heard an avalanche starting and they cut their way out in a rush, because it was the quickest way."

Laura looked up at him with a blank stare. She was trembling all over.

"I think Chaz must have done that," David said. "He heard that loud sound from earlier and he thought it was an earthquake. It might have been, you know. They make horrific sounds."

"Maybe," Laura said. Her eyes were dashing around, like she was rapidly mulling over the possibility.

"He must have panicked and cut his way out. Afraid of a tree falling on him. That must be it."

Laura leaned in and rested her head on David's chest. "Maybe you're right," she said. "He's probably close by here somewhere."

"I'll take a look around," David said. "As soon as you're ready, I'll circle the camp. He's probably dazed."

He led her to a large log that he'd placed beside the fire pit. While she sat watching, he opened the supply pack and found the coffee kit. "This will work wonders," he said, as he lifted the bag containing the ground coffee. Laura smiled back at him.

"Sorry to be such a wuss," she said. She turned her head to look out toward the trees, causing several exquisite, curly locks to tumble from her shoulder. "But I'm scared."

"No wonder!" he said. "It hasn't been the greatest morning, so far." He looked downward, not wanting her to see the worry in his own eyes. He reached down to grab some branches and dry leaves and tossed them over a large log that still smoldered from the night before. He jabbed the pile with a stick, and several small flames began twirling and flickering around the edges of the log. "Coffee always works wonders," he repeated.

"David," she said, her voice taking on the tone of a small girl. "There's something I need to tell you. Sometimes they eat people."

He was pretty sure he had it figured out. In the twenty minutes he'd spent sipping coffee and staring quietly into the fire next to Laura, he was pretty certain he knew exactly what was happening. Chaz and the other men had conspired to create this whole scene. Who knew how long they'd been creating experiences like this to convince Laura that Sasquatch really existed. David was now certain that Chaz had informed the other guys about the location of the expedition, and they had undoubtedly gone ahead to set up some equipment to stage this scene. How difficult would it have been for the men to set up specific coordinates where this would all take place? Now that he thought about it, it was clear that Chaz had been steering them toward this location in subtle ways. David remembered several occasions when Chaz had suggested that they make certain corrections to avoid rough-looking terrain, or he'd suggested that they travel a certain direction to more easily cross a river. And David had no doubt that old man Wythe was in on this, as well.

He wouldn't tell Laura, just yet. Once she realized what was really happening, she'd have to face the fact that her career had been a sham, and that the people she'd worked with for years had lied to her. She'd been made a fool of by people she trusted. How could he break that to her? The first thing he needed to do was find evidence to support his theory. He'd collect proof that Chaz and the others had concocted this entire ruse, and present it to Laura at a time when she felt less vulnerable. For now, David planned to play along with whatever happened, and be supportive and protective of Laura. Everything was making sense.

"Are you good?" he asked, as he wrapped an arm around Laura's shoulder and squeezed her close to him. "Mind if I go take a look around?"

"I think you should," she said. "I'm really worried about Chaz."

David gave her another hug and kissed her on the fore-head. "I won't go too far," he said. "Just shout if you need anything at all."

Laura nodded in return, and David stood and scanned the trees around them. To his left, he knew there was a steep drop off, so there was no point in heading that way. He decided to examine the area where he'd first been hit with a rock, that morning. If the culprits had used any sort of wheeled vehicle to transport their equipment, and they must have needed some heavy equipment, then David should be able to find some kind of tracks or indentations. He made sure to keep Laura and the fire within eyesight, turning every few steps to make sure he didn't get disoriented. He knew how easily people could get turned around in the woods, even those with decades of experience.

Nothing seemed out of place. He wasn't exactly an experienced woodsman, but he could see no disturbances in the undergrowth that would indicate anything amiss. He walked slowly, circling their camp, looking for any sign of footprints or flattened grass patches. He was nearly half way around the camp when he stopped to listen. Some pattern of sound stood out from the other noises of the forest. He waited, and then he realized what had caught his attention. There was a rhythmic tapping sound that seemed unnatural. He stopped to lean against a tree and stood still, trying to discern the direction of the sound. A slow, steady *tap, tap, tap,* sound seemed to come from his right. He walked a few yards in that direction, looking back to keep the camp in his viewing range. He realized that he was now standing several yards behind the place where Chaz's tent was situated, and through the bushes, he had a view of the gaping hole. It dawned on David that he should have started from this location. He'd need to look around that tent to see if he could find Chaz's tracks. All around him, the forest floor was shadowed in deep, red tones. His thoughts were interrupted by a heavy raindrop that hit him on the back of the arm. He swiped his arm across his shirt, and felt another drop on his shoulder. He put a hand up and swiped at the wet spot, and realized that he must have injured himself, since his fingers were then covered with blood. But he knew he wasn't injured. *What the hell?* he thought. Before he could make sense of it, another drop on the arm made him realized that the drops were coming from above him. He looked upward, and fell straight to his knees. The tree, the leaves, everything around him was covered in blood. Above him, the red-smeared body of a man was wedged between two branches. The arms and legs were gnarled and twisted into an impossible pose that made his appendages seem like extensions of the branches. He could tell that the body was most likely Chaz's, since there was a clean patch of flannel shirt material that David seemed to recognize. He couldn't be sure, however, since there was no head connected to the body.

## 23

## LOGIC

"It had to be a mountain lion," David said. "I heard once that leopards do that. They drag their kill up into trees and stash them there. They go back for it later." David recognized that he was babbling his words, but he couldn't help himself. His nerves had never been pushed to this extent, and his whole body was vibrating with fear. He was gripping Laura's gun with both hands, keeping one finger resting on the trigger. His eyes darted around from tree to tree as he scanned the shadowy landscape around them.

"We can't leave him there," Laura said, as she wiped the tears from her cheeks.

"We can't stay here," David said. "And he's too high to reach. I think we just need to mark the location and send somebody back. How far are we from a town?"

Laura glanced toward Chaz's tent. "The GPS is on his watch," she said. Her voice cracked as she spoke, and another stream of tears fell down her cheeks. "Oh, God. I hope he's not wearing it."

"Come with me," David said, swinging the gun around as he stood, pivoting on his foot like a little boy imitating a bad

Western movie actor. "We'll search his tent. We need to stick together, in case that thing comes back."

Laura stood and grabbed David's elbow. He felt her tight squeeze on his arm as he led her toward Chaz's tent. "It's orange," Laura said. "The watch."

"You go in. I'll keep a lookout."

Laura ducked into the tent and David continued to scan the area around them. He could hear Laura tossing things around inside. A crack of a branch made him jump, and the gun nearly fell from his hands. *Some hero I am,* he thought. He could barely keep his grip on the weapon. His hands were sweaty and shaky.

"Found it," Laura called from inside. "Thank God." She emerged from the tent with the device in her hand, and began thumbing away at its controls as soon as she regained her balance. "He taught me to use it in case anything happened." Her words came out in high pitched squeaks. "I can't believe he's gone."

David wrapped his arm around her shoulders again. "Don't even think about it, now. Let's just get to safety and send somebody back to get him. I think we should put it out of our heads and concentrate on staying safe, for now."

"It's still at least a full day's hike to any road," Laura said, still pressing away at the tiny buttons. "Or we could go the opposite direction and get to a pretty remote lake on the other side of that mountain." She gestured to the East with her eyes. "There could be campers there. With phones. But there's no guarantee."

"I think that sounds risky. Let's head for the road and try to make good time. Let's gather the essentials and head out," David said. "Before it comes back."

"David," Laura said. "You know that wasn't a mountain lion."

"Not now, Laura." Whatever had killed Chaz and stuffed his body in a tree was a monster, alright. But David wasn't sure what kind of monster—beast or human—he was dealing with, and he wasn't ready to discuss it.

"But there are things you should know," she said. "I'm pretty sure they're going to follow us."

"Why would you say that?" he said. "Based on what?"

"Based on my gut. I feel like they will come after us next."

"You're not being rational, Laura," David said. "We need to head for civilization."

## 24

## OBSERVATIONAL EVIDENCE

A pparently, Laura talked a lot when she was scared.

They'd been hiking nonstop for three hours, and, at first, they'd walked in silence. David had been concerned that Laura was suffering from psychological trauma. He'd tried to get her to talk a few times, asking questions as she checked the GPS watch to make sure they were staying on track to get to civilization as quickly as possible. He felt the need to keep her alert; otherwise, he noticed that she'd start to sink into a zone—staring straight ahead, big-eyed and silent, slipping further inside herself. And under these circumstances, that could be dangerous. They needed to stay sharp. David had decided to confess that he'd never actually read her book past the foreword, and that confession had seemed to transition Laura into another zone, completely. Since then, he hadn't heard more than fifteen seconds of silence. Laura had decided to fill him in on the entire content of her book in nervous whispers, filling him in on all the graphic details he didn't want to know. It wasn't exactly comforting to him. She'd spent the entire time explaining that the events of the morning were very indicative of an aggressive, aggravated Sasquatch clan. Dr. Whythe had predicted that the creatures they would encounter might be a little more dangerous than the run-of-the-mill primate, she explained. They're more intelligent, and more capable of scheming and planning. She hadn't been too concerned at the beginning of the expedition, since she'd had several brief encounters before, and nothing terrible had happened. But it was possible, she agreed, that because the creatures were running from the fires to the South and experiencing a loss of habitat, they could be abnormally irritated by encounters with the human species that caused all the habitat destruction. They were intelligent enough to make the connection.

"Do you recognize those flowers?" David had asked at one point, trying to change the subject. His ploy didn't work. She shook her head briefly and continued on her Sasquatch lecture. The whole situation was surreal and terrifying. David didn't know what to believe, at this point. Something terrifying was happening in these woods, but he'd rather not dwell on it at the moment. He'd much rather wait to make up his mind about the whole thing later, once he had the luxury of calm and clear thinking. At the moment, his brain was operating in survival mode. But he'd decided to let Laura go on and on, explaining things to him in great detail, since it appeared to keep her busy and alert. She had a purpose at the moment, so it was less likely that she would withdraw from phycological trauma. He'd actually read somewhere that physical exercise was good for helping the brain deal with a shocking event, so this marathon hike was, at least, a good elixir for their psyches.

Laura stopped suddenly and grabbed David's arm. "Did you hear that?" she asked, turning her body to look to the left.

"What did you hear?" He felt a chill wash down his torso, like ice water pouring over his body. "Shouldn't we keep moving?" He could hear his heart beating.

"I thought I heard footsteps. They stopped when we stopped."

"Let's keep moving," David said. He tugged at Laura's arm and started walking forward.

"I knew they'd do this," Laura said. "They stalk people. I hear it all the time." Her words were short and punctuated and her breath was shallow.

"Just keep moving, honey," he repeated, gently. He could feel the perspiration sprouting on Laura's arms and hands as he guided her, and he noticed a ring of sweat under her arms that hadn't been there earlier. "We'll be okay," he said. He had no idea whether or not that was true.

They had walked in silence for another several seconds, when David first thought he heard the sounds that Laura had referred to. He wasn't sure if it was his imagination, but it did seem like he could hear a third set of footsteps from somewhere to his left, and there was an occasional cracking sound of branches breaking in the distance. The footsteps sounded heavy, and bipedal. *It could be those guys from the plane*, he told himself. *They're still out here somewhere.*

"Can you hear it?" Laura whispered.

"It's probably that group of guys," he said. "Or a bear. I don't think the—whatever attacked Chaz—would follow us this far." He pulled the gun from his waistline and pulled back on the slide, snapping a bullet into place. "Why would it just stalk us? We're moving back to the South, where they came from." As soon as he finished speaking, he realized that he was referring to the beasts as if they were a reality. It was the first time he'd openly admitted that the existence of an undocumented woodland creature was a possibility.

Ordinarily, the quasi-admission would have thrilled Laura. She seemed unimpressed, under the circumstances. "To toy with us," she said. "Please don't fire that thing unless you really have to. You'll only piss it off with that. And he may have friends nearby."

"You do what you want," he said. "If I see anything I don't recognize, I'm shooting the shit out of it." He was actually getting pretty tired of her defeatist scenarios. All morning, he'd been listening to her explain what a hopeless situation they were in. He knew it wasn't fair or rational, but the more he entertained the notion that these creatures were real, the more he resented her.

"You won't be able to shoot one, anyway," Laura said, mostly under her breath. "You'll freeze up."

"Listen," David said, as he grabbed her by the crook of the arm and jerked her around to a face to face position. "We don't need to go at each other right now." He could hear his own voice quivering. "Let's please just try to stay calm. We'll get through this. Let's not be at each other's throats."

"What's that sound?" Laura said. She didn't look at him; her gaze was darting from place to place.

David stopped breathing to listen. He could hear it, too. He'd heard a similar sound on his grandfather's farm, plenty of times. Despite his grandfather's many threats, he'd teased the big, Red Angus bull every chance he got, running it to the point of exhaustion, tormenting it until it snorted for air. The heavy in-and-out breathing of the bull was similar to what he was hearing now—but the sound he heard right now had a gurgling, puffing wetness. "What the fuck?" he whispered. He looked to Laura's left side, the direction where the footsteps seemed to have come from.

Laura ignored him. She was gazing over his shoulder. "Be still," she said. Her words barely audible.

He ignored her and wheeled around to look behind him. The vision that met his eyes shattered everything he'd ever known about the world.

In front of him, about thirty feet away, was an enormous animal, humanlike in appearance, standing upright and staring back at him, breathing slowly, making a sound like inflating and deflating a tractor tire. He wanted to believe that this thing was a joke; somebody in a costume, playing the best practical joke ever. But now he understood what he'd heard so many times, from Laura and her friends. He knew that there was no way this living, breathing thing was any kind of trick. The creature's every muscle was visible on the lean body. Its face was twisted into an angry scowl, and his head was sunken into his chest, so there was no visible neck. The shoulders were easily four feet wide, and the beast had the girth of a mini van. It was clearly a male, and its body was covered sparsely with reddish brown hair. It was so tall and so unbelievably strange that it defied everything he knew about science. David couldn't move. Reality was shattered.

"Be still," Laura whispered so quietly that David wasn't sure if he'd imagined it. She didn't have to say so, anyway, since he was unable to move. His mind flashed back to a time in his youth when he'd tormented a barn mouse. He'd chased it and chased it until it was trapped in a corner with no way out. Finally, the poor thing just gave up and froze there, and stared back at him with the same gaze that David felt on his own face, at this very moment. Like the mouse, David was waiting for the cruel giant before him to decide its fate.

He tried to whisper back at Laura, but no words would come.

"*Uhff.*" The sound came from the animal.

David couldn't even move his eyes. He wanted to move his gaze away from the menacing, paralyzing eyes of the creature, but he was frozen into place.

And then it stepped away, into the darkness of the woods.

In one graceful movement, the animal disappeared behind a clump of high bushes. David kept staring at the place where it once stood, and neither he nor Laura moved until he was brought back to reality by a pain in his arm. He realized Laura had dug her nails in, deep. Slowly, he was able to pull his arm from her grip. He wrapped both arms around her and they stood in an embrace, both of them trembling.

"Do you believe me now?" Laura whispered.

# THE SEARCH

"**D**o you believe me now?" Melanie asked, as she twisted Josh's forearm around to show him the small bump resting under his skin, just below his elbow. "I'm positive that's a tracking device. Feel it. It moves around."

"I don't think I'm there, just yet," Josh said, as he poked at the small lump with his finger. "I pulled a tick off my leg yesterday. Ew, what if it's one that's burrowed under my skin?"

"Would you rather it be an alien tracking device or a bug?" Melanie said, in her motherly, chastising voice. Then her face scrunched up to an empathetic frown. "But, honestly, Josh. You should take this more seriously. You need to realize how dangerous your little game is. I'm scared for you."

In truth, Josh had been menaced by thoughts of the weird dream he'd apparently shared with Randy. For the life of him, he couldn't explain how he and Randy *both* had experienced the dream of being surrounded by little creatures who interrogated Josh about his feelings of empathy.

*What a weird concept*, he thought. He'd concluded, at first, that maybe he'd talked in his sleep, and Randy had either eavesdropped, or picked up on Josh's words, subliminally. Then Josh realized that the notion was impossible. For the past few weeks, Josh had been recording himself as he slept. He'd started strategically placing a recorder in the corner of his tent, so he could record any strange noises that might occur in the night. All he ever got on the recorder were shuffling sounds, faraway muffled noises that were indistinguishable, and a few groans. The odd dream incident was a mystery that Josh couldn't figure out, despite all of his years of studying the mind.

"I'll be okay," he said to Melanie. He was touched that she seemed to care so much. This must be how normal families operate, he thought. He wanted to say more, but he was distracted by the sound of his name being mentioned from somewhere in the distance. Melanie seemed to hear it, too, since they both looked up at the same time. Several yards away, Randy was huddled with Chet. The two men seemed to be engaged in a serious discussion. "Everything okay?" Josh yelled. When they turned to look toward him, Josh could tell that the rancher seemed pretty distraught. He grabbed Melanie by the elbow, and they both approached the pair.

"We're missing another calf," Randy said.

"Oh, man," Josh said. "I'm sorry." He felt bad for Chet, but he thought it was endearing, how Randy said "we," as if he considered himself a part of the homestead.

"Uh oh," Melanie said. "How can we help?"

"I'd like for us to spread out over the property for a search, if you all don't mind," Chet said. "It could have wandered off, although I doubt it."

"I'm in," Josh said. "Just let me know what you want me

to do." He actually looked forward to pitching in. Over the weeks, he'd had a few opportunities to help the old guy feed some of his livestock and run some of the farm equipment. It wasn't like there was a lot to do during the day, so he was interested in learning how the place worked. He'd quickly finished all the books he'd brought along to read, so the occasional chore was welcomed.

"I'd appreciate it if you could cover that area of the woods over there," Chet said, as he pointed toward a patch of trees on the far side of the grazing field. "We're looking for a little brown feller just like them others in the distance. You'll want to walk outside the fence line to avoid the bulls. Randy and Melanie can search the back fields, if they don't mind." The rancher looked around to make sure everyone was in agreement.

"Sounds good," Josh said. His search area was well in the distance, but he enjoyed the excuse to explore more of the property. And there was nothing better than a walk in the woods to help sort his thoughts. Over the past day or two, Melanie had informed him that he was still being too rigid in his beliefs. He could see her point, because he'd promised her to be completely open minded about what was happening on the ranch, but he just couldn't see any middle ground when it came to belief in aliens. You either embraced the notion, or you thought it was ridiculous, as Josh did. He just couldn't buy into alien talk.

On the other hand, Randy had pretty much convinced Josh that he was in the wrong line of work. He hadn't done it on purpose, though. Josh had spent so many hours listening to Randy's stories of places he'd seen and the freedom he'd enjoyed as a trucker, Josh couldn't help feeling envious. His job sucked. His university was small, and it didn't provide a lot of incentive or opportunity to conduct a lot of research, so he spent his time delivering the same lectures over and over, and grading mediocre papers. Then there was the constant harassment from Crystal. The past few weeks had proven one thing: his old life was pretty joyless.

He made it to the tree line where the brush grew denser, and wandered from place to place, studying the ground. Now that he was up close, he realized that the trees seemed to grow in small patches, with the occasional boulder protruding from the ground. He hadn't encountered any signs of a wayward calf, or a dead one, even, so he decided to sit on a rock and think about life as a trucker. How nice it would be, to witness these wide open spaces and bright stars on a regular basis. He had pretty much made his decision. He was quitting his job.

A movement caught his eye, about twenty yards away. It was a brief glimpse that left an odd impression in his head. Something long and stick-like had been protruding from behind a tree trunk, and it moved quickly out of sight when Josh set eyes on it. It looked more like a walking cane than a calf, but Josh was out here to investigate, so he felt obligated to check out whatever was moving behind the trees.

"Hello?" he said as he stood up, but there was no response. He walked slowly, expecting an animal, or maybe even a person, to come into view. As he moved closer to the tree, he saw a rustling in the bushes further away. Whatever it was must have slipped away. He walked all around the tree where he'd seen the movement, but nothing was there.

He wondered if the long, slender thing he'd glimpsed could have been some part of a cougar—like a tail. It thrilled him a little to think that there could be a mountain lion lurking out here in the trees. He'd never seen one in the wild before. He pictured the stick vision in his head again, to try to match the image in his head to any part of that animal, when a new, menacing thought crept into his mind. He *had* seen that shape before. It was in his dream, when he was surrounded by the beings who were observing him. The shape—the movement he'd just witnessed was dreadfully familiar; the image resembled the long, twig-like extremities of the creatures who had surrounded him and interrogated him about his emotions. Josh felt his chest tighten, and he struggled to breathe. He needed to get out of these woods and back to a place of safety.

He ran. He kept running until he was in the open field again. His lungs burned, but he kept running until he spotted Melanie, Randy, and Chet on the far side of the ranch house. He fell to his knees once he reached them, exhausted from the run. He could feel the small group staring at him. "Sorry, guys," he said. "I think I just spooked myself." He laughed in embarrassment. He wondered if they heard the tremor in his voice.

"You gave us a pretty good scare, too," Chet Skylar said. "We've been looking all over for you. Where'd you go?"

"Not too far into the woods," Josh said, trying to catch his breath. "Just beyond the tree line over there."

Randy stared back at him and wrinkled his forehead. "Kid, we looked all over them woods for you. We been searching for two hours."

At first, Josh thought Randy was joking with him. He smiled back at him, but the man returned his look with one of deep concern. As he looked at Melanie and Chet, he could see that they, also, gazed back with expressions of concern, and maybe a bit of annoyance.

"Seriously," Melanie said. "This isn't funny. Where were you?"

Josh tried to make sense of the situation. He couldn't figure out why everyone was making such odd claims, but he didn't have an opportunity to respond. Before he could say anything, he felt the vice-like pressure of Randy's fingers gripping his upper arm. The man's face was contorted, and his eyes were staring back toward the woods where Josh had just emerged. Josh turned around to follow Randy's gaze, and the sight was so strange that Josh was almost amused, at first. He thought he might be looking at some kind of strange, makeshift, skinny scarecrows. Then the reality set in. It dawned on him, that standing on the edge of the wood line, were three, grey-white beings with huge black eyes. Their stick-like arms and legs were exactly like those that Josh had seen many times before, he realized. These were the creatures that Josh had seen hunkered in the corner of his tent when he opened his eyes in the middle of the night. One of the creatures raised its twig-like arm and held up a spidery, white hand. It was the last sight that Josh could remember before complete blackness.

## 26

# KNOWLEDGE

He was back in the woods again. He walked around the bush, to see what the strange, stick-like image was, and he saw them. He knew, at that moment, that he's seen them many times before. There were three of them, and they stood there, where they had been waiting for him. One of them grabbed his hand, and through telepathy of some kind, it showed him a memory, of his first night on the ranch. That night, they had taken him to a place, and tied him down on a table. There was another table beside him, and something else was on that table. He turned to look closer. It was one of the gargoyle things that he'd seen in the tree, only now Josh realized that it was much larger than he'd thought before. It was the size of a large child. It noticed that Josh was looking its way, and it began to rise up. It wasn't tied down, like Josh. It started coming closer, and it was standing beside him, now, just a few inches away. The thing seemed to be curious about Josh. Its face hovered over him, looking down. Looking closer now, getting so close to Josh's face that he could smell what must have been its breath, as the hideous face hovered inches from his own. It had the sickly, wrin-

kled skin of a dead lab rat and the bulging eyes of a house fly. Josh
tried to scream, but the only sound he could make was a low
squeal that came from deep in his throat. Josh heard the sound of
something else approaching. The creature must have heard it, too,
because it scrambled back to its place on the other table. One of
the stick-like humanoids approached. It was holding a small cage,
and inside the cage was a small, winged creature. But, at the
same time, Josh felt like he was inside the cage, like he was the
creature. Then he realized. These creatures had taken a part of
him and mixed it with the gargoyle. They used parts of him and
mixed it with that flying creature—they used his DNA to grow a
new monster.

"YOU CAN'T LEAVE LIKE THIS," Melanie said. Her voice
sounded frantic, but Josh didn't care. He had to get off the
ranch, away from this insanity. Melanie tugged at his arm as
he stuffed his final belongings into his duffel bag. "I felt this
way, too," she said, "when I first realized they were real. You
need to stay with us, Josh, at least for tonight. You're in no
shape to drive."

He didn't give a shit what she thought at the moment.
Ever since he'd laid eyes on those—things—earlier, he'd had
flashbacks. He suddenly remembered all the things they'd
been doing to him while he thought he was sleeping in the
tent. Horrible things, that no human should ever have to
endure. They were downloading images into his head, and
they were things Josh didn't want to see or know.

They showed him something horrible about David. Josh
had no idea if the terrible scenes they showed him were real
or not, but he knew that he needed to get to David, to make

him call off his own experiment, before it was too late. There were things in the woods with David. Josh had to get to him, to warn him.

Melanie was following Josh to his car, now. He knew she meant well, but there was just no way he was going to spend another night in this godforsaken place. He couldn't risk seeing them again, not even for one night.

"I'll be fine," Josh said as he tossed his duffle bag into the back of his car.

"But, honey," she said. "If you stay one more night I'll sit up with you, I promise. I don't think you're in any shape to make a long drive."

Josh turned around and wrapped his arms around Melanie. "I'll be in touch," he said. "I promise." He waved at Randy, who was staring from a distance, and climbed into his car. He'd never been so happy to leave a place, but he wasn't sure where he was headed. He'd just drive until he found a place to stay, then try to track down David and convince him to go home. The last he heard, David was heading out West somewhere with the Bigfoot lady, but Josh wasn't sure where. Jerry might know. He'd call Jerry.

He was driving too fast, he realized, especially since he was only using one hand to drive. With the other, he was searching his contact information, trying to call Jerry. The road was curvy and it was winding up a hill, so he needed to pay more attention to his driving. He slowed down for a curve, but he still took it a little too fast. As soon as he made it around the bend, he saw that something was standing in the road, right ahead of him. It was one of the grey creatures. It had been waiting for him.

Josh slammed on the brakes, but before he could bring the car to a stop, he felt himself floating. Then he felt his body lifting upward. So much information was coming to him, now. He knew where to find David. He saw what was after David. Josh had to go find his friend.

## 27

# REVELATION

They'd walked slowly for a long time, after first seeing the beast in the path. They'd crept along in silence, listening at every step for the sound of twigs breaking and branches moving on either side of them. After a while, they'd sped up their pace to a trot, and for the past two hours, they'd kept a pretty steady run. It's amazing how motivating fear can be.

"I need water," Laura said, as she grabbed David's hand to slow him down. David slowed his pace and finally came to a stop as she tugged at him. "I can't go any further."

"Okay, okay," he whispered, as he swung his backpack around to his side and dropped it on the ground. "I don't think there's much left, though." As he pulled the canteen from its pouch, he realized the vessel was much lighter than he'd expected. He handed it over to her. "Drink what's left," he said.

Laura turned the canteen up and brought it down again, quickly. "That was only a sip!"

"I'm sorry!" he said. "I didn't realize it was so low." He felt a twinge of guilt when he saw the redness in her face. In their rush to leave the camp, he'd neglected to fill it up. They'd been moving steadily since they'd fled the camp site, and neither of them had been thinking straight under the circumstances. It was a stupid mistake on both of their parts. They'd let their water supply run out. "I guess we're going to have to look for some," David said. "We've got a good bit of distance to go, still. Shit."

"It's okay, babe," she said as she looked at the GPS watch, which slid loosely down her arm as she lifted it. "There's a stream at the bottom of the next gorge. But I'll need to rest here for a few minutes. I'm dizzy."

David looked around the woods that surrounded them. "Maybe we'll be lucky, now. I haven't heard anything following us, have you?"

"No," she said. Her expression wasn't overly reassuring, though. He could see worry in Laura's face. Now that he took the time to pay more attention, he could also see the dark semi-circles under her eyes and white around the edges of her mouth.

"Let's sit," he said, although he didn't *want* to sit. More than anything, he wanted to run like hell until he reached some sign of civilization.

Laura collapsed on the ground at the invitation. David sat cross-legged beside her, although he couldn't keep his eyes from darting all around them. "So I guess I owe you an apology," he said. "For not believing you."

Laura looked like she was attempting to say something, but it was clear she was struggling to hold back tears. Finally, she put her hands over her face and sobbed. "Poor Chaz," she said. "I never dreamed that would happen."

David moved closer beside her and wrapped his arms around her. "Don't do this to yourself. There's no way you could have known."

"But that's just it," she said. "I knew it was going to be dangerous. And I've heard of that—tree thing before. It doesn't happen often, but I've heard of it happening, like it's some kind of warning to humans, I think. I just got too cocky." She was crying, but no tears were coming out.

"Don't do this," David said.

"It's even in the book you never read." She wiped an arm across her nose.

"Oh, baby," he half laughed. "We all got ourselves into this mess. We were all cocky. Chaz included. He's been with you a long time, hasn't he?"

She nodded.

"Look," he continued. "Let's make our way slowly to the water. I'm sure we're going to be okay, now. I can feel it."

"We don't have much choice but to keep going," she said. She nudged him and pushed herself slowly to her feet. "You may have to stop me from falling. I'm still light headed." With that, her legs appeared to give out again, and David caught her by the shoulder to guide her back to a seated position. "You can't go on like this," he said. "Maybe I need to go find water and bring it back."

"No way in hell you're leaving me here alone," she said.

"Then tell me what to do," David said. His patience could be stretched only so far, and they were in a true life or death situation. "I'm kind of at a loss right now."

"Hang on." She unzipped her backpack and began dumping the contents in a pile. "I threw a bunch of random stuff from Chaz's bag in here. I might have a—*Aha!*" She pulled a small, single serve tin of green beans from the bag, and lifted it above her head like a trophy. "This will help."

"Thank Jesus," David said. "I think I have an opener." He rummaged through his own bag until he found the small, multi function gadget he'd packed in his own bag. He had a brief flashback to the moment he'd purchased the small device. He'd stopped on his way home from a lunch date with Laura, back in Ohio. It was his first purchase for this trip, and it followed their first kiss and the very moment when he'd really committed to the idea of spending the summer with her. Now it might be the thing to save her life.

"My hero," Laura said. David chuckled at the irony as he punched a small hole on each edge of the top. He handed it over and watched as she sucked at the hole with loud, slurping noises. Even now, in this horrible, unflattering moment, she was lovely. He had to pull his eyes away to prevent a melancholy tear from slipping from his eye, so he looked around again at the surrounding trees and boulders. "Did you hear that?" Laura asked, suspending the can in front of her mouth.

"*What*?" he said. The mere question made his blood feel icy.

"Birds. Crickets. Squirrels. That's a good sign."

"You scared the shit out of me," he said. His heart pounded quickly in his chest for a few beats, like it was recovering from a brief suspension. "What do you mean?"

"When they're anywhere around, everything stops. Even the bugs freeze in place when the creatures are nearby. It's an eerie silence like nothing else."

"Good to know," David said, feeling a flicker of irrational joy as he saw a squirrel jumping from one tree to another. He looked back at her face, now sporting a tiny drip of bean juice in one corner of her mouth, and he wondered what else she knew about this strange and terrifying world that was so new to him. He thought of the many times Laura had urged him to read her book. "I'm such an idiot," he whispered. "I don't know anything."

"I don't think we need to dwell on that, now," she said.

But he needed to know more. He realized that this was the first moment of stillness he'd had since he'd discovered Chaz's body. It was his first moment to acknowledge that everything he'd ever learned through formal education— the numbers that he'd worshipped and the discipline that had been his church, in a way, had been so constrained and small, all along. His learning had been confined and limited within pre-set boundaries. Those creatures were real. And if those were real, what else could be real?

"So what *are* they?" he said.

He watched as her expression went limp and she fidgeted in the dirt beside her, making small circles of mounds. "You want me to tell you what they are?" she stalled. "They're monsters. Other people have said that, but I never wanted to admit it before. But, now—"

"Seriously, Laura." There was a desperation in him, now. "I mean, I don't have any guarantees I'm going to survive the day. I'd at least like to know what's going on before I go." He was trying to half-joke, but the words came out with a pitiful ring.

"We don't know for sure," Laura sighed. "But I can tell you what I think—*we* think. There are lots of serious anthropologists looking at this, you know." She searched his eyes as if she was ready to retract at any sign of ridicule. "You've probably heard that Native Americans have told stories about tribes of hairy men since Europeans first came into contact. And stories are their way of knowing."

"I've heard something about that," David said.

"Every single tribe, in every corner of the continent has these stories, in fact. All over the Americas, really, populations who were isolated from each other, they all talked of encountering or trading with groups of large, hairy people.

Early explorers described them, too. These things have been around for a long time, in some shape or form."

"But that thing we saw on the trail, that didn't look much like a human. I mean, it was huge."

"I know," Laura said. "It seems like some of them are more humanlike than others. And maybe they're changing. We've had reports of them getting—more primitive. And bigger."

"Like, they're regressing?"

"That's exactly what we're seeing," Laura said, haltingly. "Originally, Native Americans reported Neanderthal-like tribes that could communicate. They were primitive people who had their own languages."

"But the thing we saw earlier looked like a mix between a giant ape and a man. Like *Gigantopithecus,* maybe?"

"Correct," Laura said.

"But how is this possible? It sounds so crazy."

"We think somebody—or something—is taking human DNA and conducting some kind of regression exercise. Recreating early human and ape hybrids from thousands, or even millions of years ago. And the things they're creating don't seem all that happy to be here."

"In other words, they're creating monsters."

"Yes. Through devolution."

"But who? And why?"

"We don't know, but we know that the government knows. They're either involved, or they're hiding the truth."

THEY WERE MOVING AGAIN. They were making good time, now that Laura had recovered a bit, and the water source was now only another twenty minutes away. Something about nearing this goal, along with the constant, soothing sounds of songbirds and insects, had an uplifting effect on him. Still, David's mind remained bogged down on Laura's theory about the creatures. He'd never been a fan of conspiracy theories and simply couldn't fathom that any government could carry off such a monumental experiment. First of all, politicians weren't that smart, and secondly, they weren't that discreet. It just wasn't feasible. He didn't want to come across as doubting Laura again; he'd caused himself enough trouble doing that. He had to tread lightly, but he also had to satisfy his discriminating mind.

"Hey, Laura," he said. As he expected, she maintained her pace ahead of him. "Do you really think the government could keep a secret this big?"

She took a few steps in silence before answering. "I think they have to, David."

"What do you mean?"

This time, Laura stopped and turned around. "Whoever is conducting these experiments has technology so advanced that it's mind boggling. *That's* the big secret. Mass hysteria would break out if people knew we weren't actually the superior species. That we're really just a bunch of lab rats. Suicides, panic, riots, the works. There's no way the truth can come out."

It took a moment for her point to sink in. "Are you talking about aliens?"

"Possibly," Laura said. "Some really advanced intelligence is behind Sasquatch. That's why there's a coverup. They're smarter than us, and they're mixing human beings with— other things—for some reason. Some people think they're trying to create killing machines. I probably should have listened to them." With that, she turned to start walking again.

"Jesus," he said, as he followed behind her in silence again. As much as he wanted to be in denial, he had to face the fact that he'd been living in a bubble of make believe knowledge. Ten years of college and another decade of research now felt like a joke. He'd been fed dabbles of limited knowledge and kept blind to actual reality. His head was swimming to the point that he felt ill. What would life be like, back at the university? Would he tuck away all this newfound knowledge and proceed as normal? Or would he become one of the crazy conspiracy theory crowd that he'd always made fun of? How could he ever share this knowledge with any of his friends?

He stopped suddenly. *Josh.* He realized, for the first time, that his friend could be in really serious peril, if there was any truth to this mad notion. If any of Laura's suggestions were true, Josh could be in more danger than anybody. He needed to get to Josh, to warn him off of his study, if at all possible. "We've got to get out of here!" he said. The words came out unexpectedly. Laura just turned and looked at him.

"You okay?"

"Yeah," David said. "I'm just realizing *again* how stupid I am."

"Good," she said.

## FINDING TRUTH

The stream was cold and clear, but David knew better than to drink it without boiling it first, as much as he wanted to. The last thing they needed was debilitating stomach issues over the next few hours. He volunteered to start a fire on dry ground, while Laura splashed around in the refreshing water. It seemed like he'd known her for years, but it had barely been two months since he'd first laid eyes on her. Probably because his world had been turned upside down completely in that time. His mind wandered to Chaz's family. He had no idea how many loved ones Chaz had left behind, but he knew Laura and Chaz had been pretty close. He hated that she'd have to deal with that, once they got back home. But there was something else nagging at him, and he wasn't quite sure how to broach this with Laura. How were they going to explain his death to the authorities? David was pretty sure they couldn't tell the truth, so what were they going to say? Could they become suspects in his death? It was a possibility they'd have to talk about, at some point. But he supposed it would be best to wait until they were completely out of this ordeal, and back home, safe.

"Is it ready, yet?" Laura called from the water's edge. "This is torment! I'm so thirsty."

"It's boiling, but we need to let it cool," he said. He pulled the small metal pot from the fire, walked to the water's edge, and placed the pot in a shallow pool." This should speed things up," he said. From the corner of his eye, he saw a monkey swing from one tree to another. For a moment, it reminded him of his visits to the Cincinnati Zoo, as a child. Then the reality hit him.

"Holy shit!" he said. As he stumbled backward, his hand flipped the water pot and spilled the contents into the pool.

"What the fuck?" Laura said. "You spilled it."

"Laura," he said. "I just saw an ape in that tree over there."

Laura froze, and her face blanched to a deathly white. "What do you mean?" The words came in a choked whisper.

"Over there." David intended to point to his right, but another sight caught his eye and he forgot to point. His eyes were transfixed on an object on the far side of the stream, just behind Laura. It was a huge, spider-like creature making its way toward the water. Its eyes were fixed on her. David wanted to speak, but he could not make sound. His mind traveled back to the time in his comfortable bed, while he watched Laura interviewing a boy who saw ape-like spiders in his yard. As the creature moved closer to the water's edge, David tried to speak again. This time, words came out in a squeak. "Laura, come—come out of the water." He managed to motion with his hand, but he knew it was no use. Now there was a second creature. It dropped from a tree and collapsed into a spider crawl, in one, graceful movement. David felt his face twist into a scream. He wasn't sure whether he was actually making a sound, or if it was Laura's scream he was hearing.

The creatures had lunged at Laura, first one, and then a second one jumped in. David watched in horror, as the two creatures played out some terrifying version of tug-of-war with her body; one pulled on her leg and one had its clutches on her shoulders. Laura's mouth was twisted in a horrific gape, and her eyes were rolled back to show only whites. The scene was playing out quickly, but in a surreal, slow motion scene, all at once.

David was frozen in time and space, trying to move or speak, but he could not. He wanted to run to Laura. He might have been able to fight off the animals, but he could not force his body to move.

He felt a heavy blow to the back of his head, and the next thing he knew, he was on the ground with his mouth full of wet sand. His body was moving, and as he slid along the ground, he saw a tooth and a small stream of blood. He felt a pain in his right ankle, and he realized that an enormous hand was holding him by the foot, and he was being dragged through the dirt, face down. Now his body was moving over weeds and rocks at an unreal speed. He twisted his body around in an effort to see what was happening, and the sight made his stomach muscles spasm in an attempt to vomit. He could make out the back of the head of some large, reddish, ape-like animal. Its body seemed to be three times David's size, and the lean-carved muscles were evident beneath the hairy exterior. Its enormous arms were extraordinarily long, which was the only thing keeping David from dangling in the air like a doll. He tried to look around for Laura, but all he could see was his shirt, which was being pushed up around his neck, and the accumulation of dead leaves and twigs that built up around his head as his body traveled over the forest floor.

The sound of Laura's screams faded as David's body bounced over tree limbs and rocks. A bulky object jabbed at David's stomach, and he realized for the first time that he had a gun stashed into the belt of his pants. It was a miracle that it hadn't been dislodged yet, David thought, so he attempted to keep his body twisted to one side so that the gun would remain in place. He tried to reach down to grab it, but his right shoulder scraped over a large rock, tearing away at his clothing and skin. He saw another trail of blood forming, but he couldn't really feel the pain of this injury; he assumed the adrenaline was pumping through his body, preventing him from feeling much of anything. In another attempt, he managed to reach down and pull the gun from its pouch.

He managed to get a second hand on the gun, and pulled on the barrel slide to lock a bullet into the chamber. Twisting his body fully around, he took aim at the base of the creature's head and pulled the trigger. The bullet missed its target and hit the creature in the muscle of his left shoulder. David had a sick feeling when he saw the small puff of hair and blood burst away from the skin. It looked like just enough damage to piss of the giant creature. The ape-beast dropped David's foot and let out another of the soul-piercing screams that he'd heard in the morning. It turned to look at David with the furious scowl of a demon. David tried to control his shaking hands enough to pull back on the slide again, and just as the bullet clicked into place, the beast reached down to grab him by the head with both hands. A sudden image of Chaz's headless body flashed in David's head, and he knew that he was within a second of the same fate. As the creature straddled David's body, he realized there was one opportunity that would either buy him another minute of life, or cause him a fate worse than having his head twisted off, as the creature's enormous, gallon-sized testicles swung twelve inches from David's face. He reached the gun upward to within a few inches of the smooth, grey skin, and pulled the trigger.

Blood showered over him as one of the enormous testes shattered and flew away. Again, a scream from the pits of hell reverberated through David's body, as the animal jumped and released his head. It was only a temporary reprieve, as he felt a single hand grab him by the hair and he felt his body lifting from the ground. Instinctively, he cradled the gun in his grip, in the hopes of holding on to it long enough to get another shot in. The creature drew back his arm, while David's body flapped in the air. With a whiplashing thrust, the beast released him, thrusting him through the air with the velocity of a slingshot. In this violent thrust, the gun ejected from David's grip, but a wild shot exploded and hit the beast below the eye. David saw it falling backward as his own body hurtled through the air.

A loud whoosh expelled from his lungs as his torso hit a tree trunk, stomach first, and his head and legs wrapped around and slapped at the bark in a violent *smack*. As he hit the tree, he heard bones breaking in his body. There was a brief scraping sound as he slid to the base of the tree, and then he hit the ground with a thud. Through a bloody, red haze, he could see the giant animal slumped twenty yards away. There was a pool of blood around the beast, and he was still.

At first, all was quiet. Then, David saw a second beast, and then a third, smaller one, approaching in a spider crawl through the trees on the far side of the red beast. *Just let me die now*, David thought, but then he realized that the creatures were headed for the dying animal. They seemed to approach warily, glancing back and forth at David and the wounded creature. Once they reached him, they each grabbed a leg, and they stood up to drag the animal away into the trees. David could hear whooping sounds and howls all around him, but the sounds were fading off into the forest. Then a sharp pain sliced through his chest, and his vision went black.

## 29

## COLLEAGUES

D avid didn't know where he was. All he could see was a pinkish light in his eyes, but he couldn't make out any distinct shapes. He tried to move, and pain shot through his body, causing a surge of nausea. Then he remembered. He started trembling all over, remembering that the last thing he remembered was the attack of the giant ape-like creature and his body crashing into a tree. He heard a stirring in the dirt a few inches from his head, and he prayed that he would just die now, before he had to endure any more of the terror.

Then a soft hand brushed through his hair, pushing the blood-stiffened bangs away from his face. Someone was wiping his eyes with a cloth.

"Don't move," came a familiar voice. "Help will be here shortly."

It was a man, but David couldn't place the person behind the words. He felt it was someone he knew well, but how could it be? He could still smell the dirt of the forest. He was still tangled in his same position, with his broken body twisted around the base of a tree. Was he dreaming?

A blurry face came into view with the next swipe of his eyes, and he saw a face that he knew well. It was Josh.

"What—what are you doing here?" David said. Each word created pain to shoot from his chest through the lengths of his arms.

"Don't try to talk, buddy. You've got some serious injuries, there."

David moved his eyes downward, and quickly wished he hadn't. He saw a bone protruding from a gash in his torso. The sight caused another wash of pain to spasm through his body. "But how—" David said. He wasn't sure if he was hallucinating, because he couldn't make sense of the fact that Josh had found him at the base of a tree in the middle of nowhere. "How did you find me here?" It was an effort to push each word from his throat.

"My friends told me," Josh smiled. "Now hush."

Suddenly, a new panic rose in his chest, and he started to breath more rapidly. He was happy to see Josh, but he was terrified that the creatures would return. "Josh, it's danger-ous. There are things in the woods."

"I know," Josh said. "I know it all. It's okay. They're gone now. Help is near."

David allowed Josh's words to comfort him. He had no other choice, since he felt himself slipping back out of awareness. He looked up at his friend, but he appeared to be looking through a small pinhole, now. Josh's face was surrounded by darkness. David knew he was losing consciousness again. Through his pinhole vision, he watched as Josh walked a few feet away and picked up the gun that David had dropped, earlier. He lifted the gun over his head. David heard a loud *bang*, and then the world went dark once again.

THERE WERE VOICES AGAIN. He opened his eyes once more, and saw another face that he recognized, but he didn't know this one so well.

"Dude, you're going to be okay," he said. "Remember me? It's Kenny."

It was the guy he'd seen first at the camp meeting, and then later on the plane. He was one of the men who had been following them.

"I heard the gunfire," Kenny said. "We called the authorities from our satellite phone. They're on their way."

"Laura?" David asked.

"What about her? Do you know where she is?" Kenny asked back.

David had hoped Kenny had found her, but he didn't seem to know anything. "They took her," David said. The awful memory came back to him, and tears streamed out of his eyes.

"Don't talk no more," Kenny said. "We'll find her. You just keep calm, now. 'Til that help gets here."

## 30

# RESEARCH NOTATION

After keeping vigil for a few hours, Josh finally saw some movement in David's right hand. "About time, man," he said. "They said you'd be waking about an hour ago."

David opened one eye, but the other remained stuck shut. The open eyeball darted around the room.

"You look like some crazed, zombie doll," Josh laughed softly. "You awake in there?" He wanted to be present when David awoke; he needed to make sure his friend didn't lapse into some dark place, mentally. The man had been through so much. But he couldn't stay with David for very long, he knew.

David continued to scan the room with his single eye until his second eye popped open. "Josh?" he said. His voice was cracked and gravely.

"You're in the hospital," Josh said. "Do you remember anything?" He regretted the question immediately, as David's expression dropped and his eyes filled with tears. "I'm sorry, man," Josh added. "We don't have to think about it now. We're all just happy you're here."

"Laura?" David mouthed. The sound that came from his mouth was just a dry whisper. "Is she okay?"

"People are still looking for her," Josh said. He eyed a water pitcher on a table by the window, and moved around the room to pour a glass. He dropped a straw into the cup and lifted the end to David's parched lips. "Don't try to talk too much, just yet. You're drugged up and your body is fucked up. As a matter of fact, I want you to listen to me. I have to be kind of quick." Josh looked out at the hallway. Two men in suits hovered near the nurses' station.

David responded by lifting a single, disheveled eyebrow.

"There are a few men out there waiting for you to wake up." Josh was speaking in his lowest voice. "They keep pushing the words 'bear attack.'"

David's eye's widened. "That's not what happened," he croaked.

Josh placed his hand on David's forearm and squeezed. "I know," he said. "I saw them—those things."

David seemed to relax back on his pillow a bit. "How did you find me out there?" The words came out in a whispery wheeze.

"No time for that now," Josh half whispered. "Listen, these guys seem pretty official, like federal types. And this is starting to hit the news big time, with the TV show being involved, and all. Whatever they say, I don't want you to argue with them. Just go with it, for now. Agree with everything they say."

David nodded in agreement, but his expression made it clear that he was annoyed and confused. "But, why are they here?" he asked.

Josh could hear the two men walking up the hallway. "They don't want you talking to the press." He reached into his pocket, then slipped a note he'd prepared beneath

David's blanket. "Read this later," he said. "When Jerry comes. He's on his way."

At that moment, one of the suit-clad men poked his head through the door. "Did I hear voices in here?" he asked. He glanced around the room and flashed a brief, official smile in David's direction. Josh took this as his cue to leave the room.

## 31

## CONTRASTING CONCLUSIONS

Josh had been acting pretty weird, but he had been right about these guys. David could tell that they took themselves pretty seriously, the way they hovered above him in their suits, refusing to take a seat. After everything he'd been through in the past twenty-four hours, David had no plans to entertain an argument. These guys could think anything they wanted to think. He didn't give a shit.

"Mr. Blystone," one said. The two men looked pretty much alike, although one was wearing a black tie and one wore a blue, striped one. "I know you've been through a lot, but we need to let you know that there is an investigation ongoing."

*Investigate away*, David thought.

"At this point, we have no reason to suspect you of any wrongdoing," black tie man continued.

*Wrongdoing? What the hell was this man getting at?* David's muscles clenched.

"One of our guys found a GPS watch, not far from the place where your injury occurred. It was traceable."

"Laura was wearing that!" David croaked. "Has she been found?" Trying to speak out caused his muscles to spasm, which caused streaks of pain to radiate through his torso.

"Not at this time. We only found the watch. My point is, they noticed that somebody had left a marker at a specific coordinate. Do you know anything about that?"

"Yes," David said. It was their campsite. It was the marker to indicate where the headless body of Chaz Galliher was stuffed into a tree. His gut lurched.

"I assume you know that our men did locate the remains of a male victim at that location. We have not made official identification at this time. Did you see what happened to this man?"

"No," David said. It was true. He hadn't actually seen what happened to Chaz. "I think—," David croaked. "It looked like he was pulled from his tent."

Mr. Blue Tie spoke up. "That's consistent with our theory," he said. "When our men got to him, there wasn't much left. He was—consumed. We believe that a rogue bear attacked the individual, and then tracked you and Miss London before finally going after the two of you, one at a time." Both men stared sternly into David's eyes, as if they were daring him to speak. "Do you have any memory that would be inconsistent with this scenario?" Blue Tie asked.

"None," David said.

"Good. We don't see any reason to consider that anything criminal went on out there. Not at this time." The man flashed another syndicate smile and turned to his partner. "I think that's it," he said. The two of them nodded and left the room.

*Anything criminal.* The words reverberated in his brain. If he hadn't already seen his belief system being rocked upside down over the past few days, he would have been surprised.

These men, who seemed to represent the law or the government in some kind of way, had just fabricated a story and pressured David into playing along. And the thing was, he didn't even care. He hurt too much, inside and out, to give a damn what people thought. Besides, nobody would ever believe him, no matter what he did. That was the cruelest irony; he had finally found his way around to Laura's side, and he was left alone, now, to tell her story. And he didn't know if he'd ever be brave enough to tell it. He was just realizing how brave she was.

He moved his head slowly around the room, trying to find a clock. Someone had placed his phone on a charger, but it was on the bedside table, and David knew it would be too painful to reach for it. He looked to his side, and realized that there was a TV remote attached to his bed rail, just within finger reach. He managed to press the button to bring the screen to life. To his relief, a news anchor appeared on the screen. He wanted to know if this was hitting the news, yet. It wasn't long before he had his answer. After a few minutes of political updates, the anchor began announcing the news of the day.

*We're still following a story out of California, where we're hearing that a crew from the popular cable television show,* Sasquatch Encounters, *has suffered a tragic encounter with an animal, and police are saying that this was an attack from an apparent rogue black bear. Initial reports are that the attack has resulted in at least one fatality, but it's not clear who the victims are. We do have reports that Laura London, the star of the show, was present on this apparent expedition, but we have no specifics on her condition. The crew was accompanied by a university professor, Dr. David Blystone, of Gratis, Ohio. Dr. Blystone is in critical condition.*

*Good god*, David thought. His family must be terrified. He

tried to reach for his phone, but the pain took his breath away.

"Can I help you with that?" a voice came from the doorway. Staring back at David was the goofy face of Jerry Price.

## 32

# THE FINAL SAY

"What the hell are you doing here?" David managed to croak. He'd discovered that it didn't hurt to talk quite so much if his head remained perfectly still.

"I wasn't actually that far away when I read about you on Facebook," Jerry said as he settled into a chair and gazed upward at the television attached to the wall. "I see it's all over the news."

David rolled his eyes and nodded. "So where were you? When you heard?"

Jerry looked uncomfortable, like he was trying to think of what to say next. "I was actually in New Mexico yesterday. I caught an early flight to get here."

"Why?" David said. Jerry's face was uncharacteristically serious. He was usually the one to find humor in every situation, so his vibe was unsettling.

"You doing okay?" Jerry seemed to avoid the question.

"No," David said. "Not really. But I appreciate you coming here." He wondered if there was any way that he could tell Jerry, or anybody other than Josh, about what had really happened.

Jerry stared at David with wide, searching eyes, like he had something big to say, but couldn't make the words come out of his mouth. "Listen, man. There's some stuff I need to tell you, before anybody else gets to you. I need to start with Josh." Jerry was sitting on the edge of his chair, now, with the nervous look of a child who was about to confess something.

"Yeah, he seemed a little odd when we spoke," David said.

"Oh," Jerry said, looking a little perplexed. "I don't know when that was, but yes, he's been acting really odd for a while. He actually told Crystal to stick her job up her ass."

David tried to stifle the painful laugh that tickled at his throat. "That's been a long time coming," David said. "Good for him."

"David, Josh is dead."

For a moment, David stared at Jerry's face to see if he was joking. Surely, even Jerry wouldn't joke about a thing like that under these circumstances. "No, he is not," David said. "And that's not funny."

"It's true," Jerry said. He was actually tearing up a little. "I didn't want to have to tell you like this, but I knew you'd find out as soon as you picked up your phone. They've sent out an announcement to our work email. I'm really sorry to do this, after all you've been through."

David laughed softly and shook his his head slowly from side to side. "There's been a mistake," he said. "He's here in the hospital, or he was a minute ago. In fact, he told me you were coming."

Jerry's face was stone white. "David, listen to me. That's why I was in New Mexico. I went with Crystal to identify the body."

A cold chill crept through David's body. Jerry was really

serious. *The drugs*, he thought. He'd heard about strong pain medication causing hallucinations. He must be on some powerful-ass drugs. "You're really sure?" he asked. He thought back to his conversations with Josh. Could he have imagined all that?

"I'm sure. Someone saw his car going off a cliff. He went off the road into a river. Skid marks on the road seemed to indicate that he swerved to avoid something. I had to fly out to help Crystal with the identification." Jerry's demeanor changed. "That bitch was more annoyed than distraught, though. I swear, I've come to hate her. Do you know they were related—Crystal and Josh?"

"What?" David said. He was still in a numb fog. "I guess that makes sense, now that I think about it. She always acted weird about him." He was still trying to remember his full conversation with Josh.

"Well, she's pissed about our little experiment and afraid everyone will find out he was out chasing UFOs and you were out chasing Bigfoot. And now everything is all over the news. She's such a *bitch*. Damage control, that's her main concern. In fact, she could have come with me to see you. She was with me when I read the news about you, but she just flew home."

"Kind of you to come," David said. The word *dumbstruck* went through his head. Now he knew the real meaning of that word, because that's exactly how he felt. Then his eyes moved to his drinking straw. The one Josh had placed in his water cup, about fifteen minutes earlier. *Could that have been a nurse?*

"You going to be okay?" Jerry said. "I probably should have waited."

"Jerry," David said. "Will you do me a favor?"

"Sure."

"Will you come over here and pull back my blanket? See if there's a piece of paper there."

Jerry scooted around David's bed, sidestepping all the way, keeping two disquieted eyes on David. "*Okayyy*," he said. He reached David's far side and lifted the corner of his blanket. Just as David had suspected, there was a white piece of paper there, folded into quarters. Just where Josh had left it.

"Can you read that out loud?" David asked.

Jerry unfolded the paper and looked down at the scrawled message. His face scrunched up on one side, in apparent confusion. "It says, 'I had to do Crystal's damned job. She's such a slacker.'"

David began to chuckle, and then his chuckle turned into a horrifically painful, excruciating, totally involuntary laugh.

"I don't get it," Jerry said.

"Jerry," David said. "Do you remember back at the conference, what Crystal was supposed to do? When we first made all these plans?"

"What do you mean?"

"Jerry, dude," David tried his best to stop laughing, since it hurt like hell. "It was Crystal's job to discover the truth about ghosts."

## 33

# THE CONVENTION SPEAKERS

Jerry realized this would be the largest group he'd ever addressed, in all his years of lecturing. After decades of speaking in front of university students, and after making dozens of conference presentations over the years, it was hard to believe that he could still get jittery speaking in front of a big crowd. But this crowd was different. Looking out from his table at the front of the enormous room, it seemed like there must have been a thousand people staring back at him. He'd had no idea that a paranormal convention could draw so many people. He laughed to himself. A year ago, he thought hooking up with David for the project would gain him some attention. He was right.

The moderator was quieting the crowd. Jerry would be the first one of the panel to make his introduction. He cleared his throat.

"Good morning, everyone." His voice boomed from the microphone and bounced off the walls of the enormous room. "My name is Jerry Price, and I'm happy to be back in Savannah." It was true. He still wanted to see that oyster shucking museum. "I will be speaking about my experience with a small creature—a demon, actually—that invaded my home and wreaked havoc on my personal life, as well as my sanity." That wasn't so bad. He got a small ripple of laughter. He winked at his son in the audience and handed the microphone to the man seated beside him.

"Greetings," the man said. "My name is Johan Nilsson, and, among other things, I will be explaining the process we used to eliminate this creature from Jerry's home. And, as always, I would like to caution you all. If, at any time during my presentation, you experience anything unusual, *please* let me know."

Jerry squirmed in his seat, as Dr. Nilsson handed the microphone to David, who was seated on the far side of him.

"Hello, everyone. My name is David, and after the year I've had, I have a drinking problem." The room erupted in laughter. Jerry was a little miffed that David had played the funny card. He was such a jerk.

"I know I shouldn't joke about that," David continued, "but I am here to talk about the tragic and extraordinary expedition—and I'm sure I don't have to explain *which* expedition I'm talking about, since it was all over the news—and I'll be talking quite a bit about the coverup that ensued. I'll address the strange visitations I received, as well as the chaos that I experienced, after I got fired from my job. I'll also talk about the stress and self-hate that came with it, and yes, a lot of self-medication." David handed the mic to the person sitting on his right.

"My name is Laura," the woman said. The audience broke out in applause. Laura smiled and waited for the adoring audience to calm down, like the show biz professional she was. "Today I welcome all questions, but I'd also like to talk specifically about my upcoming documentary, in which I focus on a special topic in the Sasquatch world, and that topic is *compassion*. As you may know, I am here with you today, only because I experienced compassion from an unexpected source. If it weren't for the mercy of one creature, a female with a small child of her own, I would not have survived the attack that took place during the infamous expedition. This creature came to my defense and protected me from the others in her clan. I believe—it is my theory—that these creatures, through DNA manipulation, are becoming more human-like, when it comes to emotions. I look forward to your questions."

"May I interject?" Doctor Nilsson said?

"Of course," Laura said, as she handed the microphone down the line.

"It is also my theory, that many of the creatures that we will discuss at this conference have been created by design, but they have started to develop something unexpected. A few have taken on this very human trait of compassion. I am sure that this is a very unintended development, but it is one that has proven very fortuitous for Ms. London, and for the rest of humanity. Human compassion, as it turns out, is hereditary. It travels through DNA. And in my next book, I will argue that it has been the saving grace of the entire human population.

After a few minutes of awed silence, the moderator addressed the audience again. "Are there any questions?" he said.

"I have a question!" someone yelled from the audience. "When is the wedding?"

In all his years, Jerry had never seen David Blystone blush so deeply. The bastard was always the center of attention.

THE END

# ABOUT THE AUTHOR

Grace Fleming is an emerging author of stories about monsters, madness, and murder. This is Grace's third book.

## ALSO BY GRACE FLEMING

Celebrity Wedding in Flowery Branch

It's Only a Story

(Free download)

Made in the USA
Columbia, SC
11 August 2019